DESDEMONA MOVES ON

DESDEMONA MOVES ON

by BEVERLY KELLER

Bradbury Press / New York

Maxwell Macmillan Canada / Toronto
Maxwell Macmillan International
New York / Oxford / Singapore / Sydney

Bradbury Press
Macmillan Publishing Company
866 Third Avenue
New York, NY 10022

Maxwell Macmillan Canada, Inc.
1200 Eglinton Avenue East
Suite 200
Don Mills, Ontario M3C 3N1

Macmillan Publishing Company is part of the Maxwell Communication
Group of Companies.

First edition
Printed and bound in the United States of America
10 9 8 7 6 5 4 3 2 1

The text of this book is set in 13 point Caledonia.

LIBRARY OF CONGRESS CATALOGING-IN-PUBLICATION DATA
Keller, Beverly.
Desdemona moves on / by Beverly Keller. — 1st ed.
p   cm.
Summary: Chronicles the comic mishaps of twelve-year-old Desdemona
and her family after they move into a luxurious new house.
ISBN 0-02-749751-8
[1. Dwellings—Fiction.   2. Moving, Household—Fiction.   3. Single
parent family—Fiction.   4. Humorous stories.]   I. Title.
PZ7.K2813Dc 1992
[Fic]—dc20   92-7127

To Judah

DESDEMONA MOVES ON

The weeks before Christmas were hectic, but not in the way they're supposed to be, not with shopping and decorating and wrapping presents. For the second time since summer, my father was busy trying to find us a place to live.

Of course, to my sister Aida and my brother Antony, Christmas was far more important than a roof over our heads. They worried so about presents that our housekeeper took matters into her own hands. Right after dinner Friday, she announced that she would take Aida shopping on condition my father take Antony. Antony had a habit of taking his clothes off anyplace when he felt upset or frustrated. I guess

Mrs. Farisee thought it was too much to risk in a crowded department store.

My father agreed. Mrs. Farisee was not a person you would disagree with lightly.

"Be sure you wrap up," he told Aida, and went on reading "Houses for Rent" in the paper.

I finished putting away the dinner dishes, with Sherman's help. Though his parents owned the house they were throwing us out of, none of us held it against him. Sherman had hung around for dinner. Usually Mrs. Farisee sent him home before dark, but maybe this day she'd been infected by the Christmas spirit.

Mrs. Farisee went to get Aida from the room the twins and I shared, but came right out and stalked into the parlor.

"Your children," she told my father, "are warped."

This was nothing new to him, but I suppose he felt obliged to go with us and see what they'd done, if only to be sure it was nothing that would cost a lot of money to repair.

Aida was standing in the middle of our room wrapped in toilet paper.

It must have taken at least a dozen rolls to swaddle her, layer after layer, so that only her nose and her eyes showed. Antony stood by, another roll in his hand, waiting for the fuss to pass over.

I knew, of course, what was going on. "They've been watching old horror movies with the sound turned off." I looked at my brother. "*The Mummy* or *The Mummy's Hand*?"

Mrs. Farisee stood in the doorway. "In my day, children did not have their own television sets in their rooms."

I could have pointed out that it was only a twelve-inch black-and-white. I could have pointed out that without a television set in his children's room, my father, who slept on the parlor Hide-A-Bed, might have had to negotiate with us in order to watch *Washington Week in Review* when a science fiction thriller was on.

I could have, but I wasn't even tempted. Pointing things out to Mrs. Farisee would be like getting lippy to the Pope.

Sherman eyed the paper swaddling my sister. "I'm glad you guys buy recycled."

While he and I unmummied Aida, Mrs. Farisee went to make herself a cup of herb tea and calm down.

Squatting, my father took Antony by the shoulders so that my brother was forced to look him in the eye. "Now. Antony. You do not make mummies out of living people."

"Or any people. Not anymore. At least not that I

know of." Sherman was an eleven-year-old walking encyclopedia.

Antony looked faintly disappointed. "You mean I have to wait until she's dead?"

"No. No." Being a psychologist, of course, my father knew you deal with children's questions about death right away, and reassuringly. "When your sister is dead . . ."

Muffled noises came from the mouth beneath the paper. We'd started unwrapping Aida from the feet up, which had seemed easiest.

My father kind of swivelled on his haunches to face Aida. "No, sweetie. No, you won't be dead for years and years."

"So when she is who will mummy her?" Antony asked reasonably.

My father turned back to him. "Nobody. Nobody."

"What, we just throw her *out*?" my brother demanded. "Even if it's not trash day?"

"We don't have to think about that now." I guess even a psychologist, after a day at work, may not be up to a pair of five-year-olds. "*Mrs. Farisee!*" he called.

"Right here."

"I'm sure Antony wouldn't take off his clothes if you took them both shopping." The man was plainly desperate.

4

"Don't push me," she said. "If I weren't a woman of my word I wouldn't take either one of them."

Unswaddling my sister took a while, since Sherman insisted on taking the paper off intact so that it could be re-recycled. My father went back to the parlor to go on reading the ads.

"Besides," Sherman told Antony as we uncovered Aida's mouth, "you don't just wrap people up to make a mummy, even when they're dead."

"You don't?" Aida asked.

Even a half-request for weird information was irresistible to Sherman. "Of course not. When a pharaoh died in ancient Egypt . . ."

"A sparrow?" Now Antony looked truly distressed.

"Pharaoh," Sherman said. "Ancient Egyptian rulers were called pharaohs."

"Rulers," Aida told her brother, while I unbound the rest of her head. "Like yardsticks."

"No, no." Sherman was patient. "Rulers, like kings and queens. Anyway, when they died, special people took out all their insides so they wouldn't rot, and then covered the bodies with more anti-rot herbs and stuff."

"I'm glad it wasn't sparrows," Antony said.

"Then," Sherman went on, "they wrapped the

5

dead pharaohs in strips of linen and buried them inside enormous pyramids."

By now, he had the twins so enthralled Aida stood stock-still while I got her coat on her.

"What's a pyramid?" Antony asked.

"A tomb," Sherman told him.

Antony was astonished. "They buried dead people inside 'toons?"

"No, no, no." There was just a slight edge to Sherman's voice, but, then, the twins could wear away anybody's patience. "Tombs, like graves."

"So then what?" Aida urged Sherman, as I put a hat on her.

Sherman was as absorbed in the subject as the twins were. "The people buried wonderful jewels and crowns and goblets and treasure with the bodies, like presents for their next life."

"You mean *in* the bodies. They'd have to put something back into them or they'd cave in." Even at five, my sister had the mind of an engineer.

"Sure," Antony agreed. "That's why they wound the bodies in cloth strips—to wrap the presents."

I shoved my sister gently from the room. "Go. Enjoy the spirit of the season."

"You get Antony ready while I find a place to stow all this toilet paper," I told Sherman.

He turned on PBS.

It is not easy tucking away reams of hastily folded toilet paper in a small bathroom.

When I came back, Antony had his parka on, his jeans tucked into his boots, and his stocking cap pulled down over his eyes and nose. I pulled the hat back so he could see and breathe.

"I'm a Teenage Mucus Ninja." He dragged it down over his nose again.

"I am not leading any smothering five-year-old Mucus Turtle through crowds of Christmas shoppers." Taking him by the wrist, I hauled him from our room.

My father was in his coat, still scanning the ads. We were at the front door when the telephone rang. I was tempted to say, "Don't answer it." Even at twelve, going Christmas shopping in the evening is a magical event.

But I thought it might be somebody calling to rent us a house.

My father didn't talk long. When he hung up, he looked stunned. "Bramwell Grove. He wants to come over."

"Here? He wants to come here?" This was like having Don Corleone phone to say he wanted to drop by. Besides the property Bramwell owned with Sherman's parents, he had a whole *empire*, from high-rise office buildings to the seedy old Rancho

Grande Mall, to whole blocks he was going to raze for a new shopping center. But it wasn't just that Bramwell was rich; it was that he had all the softness and gentleness of a Mafia kingpin.

"What about shopping?" Antony asked anxiously.

"After." My father still looked a little dazed. "First we have to see what Bramwell Grove wants."

"I'd better hang around," Sherman declared. "You don't know how tricky my uncle can be."

Even though I'd met all the Groves, I had a wild notion that the spirit of the season might have struck Bramwell, that he might have got Sherman's parents to reconsider our eviction.

It was a serious eviction, though. Our three dogs had run through the wet concrete foundation of a whole block of condominiums the Groves were building. Sherman explained to his parents that he and Aida and I had to go after the dogs, that we could hardly leave them to harden in cement, even though it did make a lot more of a mess to get them out of it.

You can't reason with some people.

The Groves gave us ninety days to move out.

It occurred to me now that maybe, Christmas or no, Bramwell was going to try to pressure us into moving right away, since his family was planning to raze our block for fancy condos.

For all his quirks, Sherman never failed to come through in an emergency. While my father and I waited for Bramwell, Sherman kept Antony interested by telling him the life history of vampire bats. There was no mistaking Bramwell's arrival. On a street of two-bedroom, one-bathroom houses you don't often hear a car come roaring up like a Grand Prix winner, *rrrruuuummmmmmm.*

Still, my father and I didn't go to the door until we heard the knock.

While Sherman's father was a handsome man, Sherman's uncle outclassed even Harley Grove. Bramwell was built like Sylvester Stallone, only taller. His hair was black and thick, and his eyes dark. I suppose a lot of women would think he was about the most gorgeous thing they'd ever seen. One of my father's ex-girlfriends, Shirley Miller, who was otherwise a smart and admirable woman, had thrown my father over as soon as she *met* Bramwell. I don't know if part of Bramwell's charm was that he was dangerous looking. There was a kind of hard, tense edge to him. Of course, the fact that even Sherman's mother called him a rich slumlord, the fact that the tenants in his own Rancho Grande Mall looked upon him with all the affection the Star War rebels had for Darth Vader, might have prejudiced me.

Bramwell strode into our parlor like a movie star arriving impressively late for a premiere.

My father didn't offer to take his coat. I could see why. Sherman's uncle didn't merely fill a room, he took it over. To take his cashmere coat and scarf would be too much like waiting on him.

"So," Bramwell greeted us. "Where are your dogs?"

Antony darted from the room.

"Those dogs are licensed! Those dogs are legal!" Sherman stood almost toe-to-toe with his uncle.

Bramwell put a firm hand on his nephew's head, as if, with just a slight pressure, he might scrunch him into the floor. "I want to see them."

For Bramwell Grove to make a social visit to your dogs was like the Internal Revenue Service sending an agent out to cuddle your accountant.

On the other hand, there was Bramwell's dog. Sherman and the twins and Shirley Miller and I had been with Bramwell when we found the most broken-down stray I'd ever seen, a dog so sick and starved he'd lost most of his hair and all his will to live.

Bramwell had kept him.

"Our animals *are* licensed," my father said firmly. "And we do not have to be out of this house until . . ."

"Look, I just want to meet them, okay? I've got nothing against mutts."

Herb and Joe and Sadie came tumbling in, my brother in their wake.

Antony had not gone to hide them. He'd gone to fetch them. I'd forgotten how thrilled he would be to have *anybody* want to meet them.

Herb and Joe and Sadie are large dogs. Even with regular brushing, the hair they shed in a week could build a fourth dog.

Herb and Joe and Sadie love company.

Bramwell Grove, in his cashmere coat and custom-tailored suit, his gold cuff links and his diamond rings, backed into the nearest chair.

"Down!" my father commanded, as the dogs sniffed Bramwell and slurped his cheek and tried to climb into the chair with him. "Sit! Stay!"

Sherman hauled Joe off his uncle while my father grabbed Sadie and I yanked Herb away.

A lesser man than Bramwell might have been shaken. But Bramwell, for all his faults, was not a lesser man.

My father kept a firm grip on Sadie's collar. "They . . . ah . . ."

"They love people," Sherman volunteered.

Bramwell eyed our dogs appraisingly. "So how are they around other dogs?"

11

"Great!" Even though it was plain that Sherman was not quite sure what his uncle was up to, he was going to defend our beasts from anything. "These dogs have dispositions . . ."

"Would they fight another male?"

"Dog?" Sherman asked. "Male dog?"

"All our animals are neutered," my father said.

"What's tutored?" Antony was hanging on to Sadie's neck.

"Neutered," my father said absently. "Fixed so they can't make puppies."

"Good." Bramwell nodded. "So they probably wouldn't fight. My dog's neutered, too."

"You want to bring him in?" Sherman asked. "Is that it? These people won't mind. These people love dogs."

"Do yours sleep in the house?" Bramwell asked, while Joe and Herb and Sadie wept and strained to kiss his hands.

"Sure," Antony volunteered.

"What do you feed 'em?" Bramwell seemed uncommonly intense for a man making idle conversation.

"The best, only the best," Sherman assured him. "I mean, these people know how to treat a dog."

Bramwell addressed himself to my father. "So you're a psychiatrist, right?"

"Psychologist," my father said.

"Okay. Same difference. You deal with people's quirks."

"We all have quirks," my father objected. "I help people . . ."

"But, I mean, you'd kind of have a sense of an animal's . . . feelings."

"Listen," Sherman told his uncle, "the man *loves* animals. He *knows* animals."

"What I came to ask . . ." For a moment, it seemed as if Bramwell Grove might be at a loss for words. "I'm wondering if you'd keep Dow Jones."

I had heard of the Dow Jones Industrial Average; on Fridays my father always watched *Wall Street Week in Review*, though it seemed odd to me that a man who couldn't afford to buy a house would be following the stock market. Still, I'd absorbed enough in walking through the parlor to know that the Dow Jones Industrial Average had to do with what stocks sold for.

"Dow Jones?" my father repeated blankly.

"That's his dog," Sherman explained. "Dow Jones."

"You are trying to give us a dog?" My father seemed stunned. "Your family is evicting us because of our dogs, and you want to give us a *fourth* one?"

"Give? This is my animal we're talking about!"

Bramwell exclaimed. "You don't give away your dog! I am only asking if you'd board him for a week. I have to go to Chicago and then New York to close a couple of deals, and I can't just leave Dow Jones in some kennel."

"Your brother has a yard," my father pointed out.

"Yeah, and they've got Jake," Bramwell countered.

I could see his point. Jake was a dog Sherman's parents had bought, four pounds of swaggering macho canine fluff.

"When we take Jake to the vet," Sherman observed dourly, "we have to put a *harness* on him so he can't attack the Dobermans and German shepherds in the waiting room."

"Besides," Bramwell said, "nobody's ever home at my brother's."

This was true. Sherman's parents were busy making money and politics all day and going to or giving parties almost every night, and when Sherman wasn't at school he spent most of his time at our house.

"They have a maid," my father pointed out.

"Yeah. A different one every two weeks," Bramwell said. "I am talking about a sensitive dog here. I took this animal off the streets. This guy has paid his dues. I'm not about to leave him with people

14

who have no feeling for his species. As it is, his world is going to collapse with me leaving for a week. You put him in some kennel, or with people who barely have time to give him more than his meals, and he's going to fall apart."

"I'm sorry," my father said. "But right now, I've got all I can handle looking for a place to live with three dogs and three kids."

"I'll pay," Bramwell said. "I'll pay double what it would take to put him in a kennel."

I could see my father waver. But he shook his head. "No. I just couldn't handle a fourth dog with all of the other pressures. Besides, our housekeeper barely tolerates these three."

Bramwell was silent. Then, like a man forced into an admission that infuriated and embarrassed him, he growled, "I don't *know* anybody else I'd want to leave him with."

And I realized that for all his money, all his power, he probably didn't have the kind of friends you'd trust with a dog.

"Have you thought of a house sitter?" my father suggested.

"I'm not going to leave him alone in the apartment with somebody who just walks him around the block a couple of times a day." Then he paused and scratched Herb's neck as if he had nothing more than a social visit on his mind.

"Have you found yourself a place to live?" he asked conversationally.

"I'm looking," my father told him.

"Time's running out. My brother's not going to give you any extension, you know." Bramwell leaned back slightly and stretched his arms. "I might have a deal for you." He was casual. He was offhand. He took out a business card, scrawled something on it, and handed it to my father. "Why don't you meet me there tomorrow morning. Ten, say."

He knew he had us.

My father waited until we heard the *rummmm-rummmmrummmm* of Bramwell's blue Maserati before he looked at the card.

Driving downtown, we didn't talk much about Bramwell. Antony wanted to know whether we thought Aida would like a mummy for Christmas. My father assured him she would not, and that mummies were not stocked in respectable department stores.

I was preoccupied, wondering what kind of deal Bramwell was talking about.

My father made us all stay with him in the stores, which meant I couldn't shop for him or Antony. Then we had to persuade Antony that purple spandex tights would not be suitable for Mrs. Farisee, and that if he bought them he'd have no more money left.

Finally, my father took us down to the coffee shop and treated us to dessert and then took Sherman home.

2

Saturday morning, Sherman was at our house right after nine. Either he was hoping to finish his Christmas shopping with us or, more likely, he was suspicious about what kind of deal his uncle was hatching.

It was Mrs. Farisee's day off, and I told my father I would fall into a raving, foaming frenzy if I didn't find out soon what Bramwell had in mind, so we brought the twins.

Sherman, of course, came with us.

As we drove past the outskirts of town, the twins asked maybe eight or ten times when we were going to finish Christmas shopping. Each time, my father assured them automatically that we'd go as soon as we finished meeting Sherman's uncle.

We drove into the hilly part of town, where handsome houses on big lots were set well back from the street. As we wound through the hills, the houses got even more impressive and the yards bigger.

The paved road gave way to gravel, and the houses were a little less imposing but further apart, with no sidewalks, no streetlights. Near the crest of a hill, the road split; one fork curved up and to the right, the other cut straight into the hillside.

The twins speculated that, since there were no other cars on the road, and no people out walking, this was the time when a UFO would land on the car and kidnap us all.

"We can't leave the dogs!" Antony was suddenly alarmed.

While I was convincing him that no UFO would make off with a car full of kids, my father announced, "This is the address."

The gravel driveway was almost as long as a city block, widening into a crushed-rock parking area where Bramwell's Maserati stood.

The house was nothing like the grand homes we'd passed. A redwood flattop with a tar and gravel roof, it sat on a level clearing cut out of the hillside. To our right, a terraced, overgrown upslope led to the road. To the left of the parking pad, the land sloped down in cascades of unkempt shrubbery to a barbed wire fence that separated it from a wide, shallow valley.

Without greeting us, Bramwell got out of the car and walked to the front entrance, key in his hand. He unlocked the front door and stepped inside.

The front door opened directly into a huge living room. The pink draperies were filthy and shredded, but the room itself was fascinating. The east wall, beside the front door, and the south wall, which overlooked the valley, were all glass, with a glass door on the valley side. The other two walls were panelled, soaring a good twelve feet to a beamed ceiling. The carpet was gray, a little worn, but clean. Separating this parlor from a small dining room was a Swedish fireplace, open on three sides.

In the back of my mind had lurked a hope that I was careful not to admit to the front of my mind . . . the notion that Sherman's uncle might be offering us a place to live. I realized now that the man had some reason I'd not suspected for bringing us here. He'd never offer us anything as glamorous as this house.

For the first time, I understood why people wanted to live in a place with a view. Through the glass south wall I could look beyond our town to the next and the next, but we were far above all the noise and smells and traffic.

"We got this place in a complicated deal," Bramwell was saying. "You could have it for the same rent you're paying."

My breath stuck below my collarbone for a second. *He was offering to let us live in this house!* And it wasn't merely a house, but a house surrounded by land, a house with twelve-foot ceilings in the parlor and a Swedish fireplace, a house that overlooked a whole *territory.*

Antony peered warily into the fireplace. "Do they cook things in here?"

Aida looked nervous. "What kind of things?"

"Big things," he declared with a kind of doomsday certainty.

When something as astonishing as Bramwell's offer occurs, you really aren't sure that it's actually happening. I guess that's why the better clichés get such heavy use—they're true.

Even though he kept his face composed, I could see that my father was as impressed as I.

"Providing," Bramwell added, "that you take Dow Jones."

My father seemed determined to play it cool. "How many bedrooms?"

"Three."

Three, I thought. That meant my father would at last have a room of his own.

"There are four in our family, plus a housekeeper," my father said, as if we hadn't been sharing a two-bedroom house for the past months.

"No problem," Bramwell said. "There's an addition."

He led us into the kitchen.

"Oh, yuck," Sherman muttered.

On my right was an eating area, one wall papered in a greasy spattered cherry print wallpaper. In front of me were two filthy windows over a sink and Formica counter. Against the wall on my left stood a refrigerator oozing brown liquid onto the gray linoleum, which was sprinkled with mouse droppings. Opposite the kitchen windows was an old gas range flanked by counters and drawers.

Bramwell did not let us linger. Striding past us, he opened the door beside the windows. "Your addition."

"*That?*" my father demanded.

The room was less an addition than an afterthought. It measured no more than six by eight feet, and it had three doors—one from the kitchen, one to a small fenced gravel yard outside the kitchen windows, one to the garage.

Bramwell showed no embarrassment. "A bed

would fit in here. Maybe a dresser, or a desk. Even a chair, if you kept it under the desk. Here, come here."

We followed him into the garage. It was a cemetery for junk—rusty bedsprings, moldy mattresses, seatless three-legged chairs, stacks of damp newspaper.

Bramwell opened a narrow door. "And you've got your john."

My father stared at the tiny windowless cubicle, which held a toilet and a sink.

"Neat." My sister had overcome her qualms about the fireplace—or maybe she was just eager to settle the deal and go Christmas shopping.

Bramwell strode back through the addition and the kitchen, skirted the dining room, and hurried us down the hall.

On the left were two big bedrooms. Like the living room, their south walls were all glass, with glass doors. It didn't strike me as the most secure of arrangements, but I told myself we had nothing to fear from prowlers. Besides three dogs and my father, we had Mrs. Farisee. I could not imagine even the most reckless criminal standing up to our housekeeper.

Both bedrooms had stained, shredded, pea green draperies on those window walls. It occurred to me that the former tenants either kept panthers or had very, very active house cats. The floors were interesting. The house seemed to have been constructed with whatever was handy. The kitchen floor was gray linoleum. The addition was floored in tan asphalt tile, the larger southern bedroom in cork, and the other in green vinyl.

Bramwell led us into a third bedroom, on the north side, a smaller room with wide, high windows and the same flooring as the kitchen.

Finally, he ushered my father into the bathroom. It was long and narrow, with a linen closet and tub on one side and a toilet and counter with basin on the other, the walls enamelled a bright blue, the floor a purple linoleum.

"The only difference from what we have now is that this place is downright eccentric," my father said.

I was appalled that a man in his position would be so negative. Or was he trying to bargain? We had never lived in a house with such a wonderful living room, whole walls of glass, a fireplace open on three sides, and a view that seemed to stretch on for town after town. And even if I got stuck with the addition, it would be a room of my own.

Trying to outcool Bramwell Grove was like trying to outeat a school of piranha. "On the other hand, it beats nothing, which is what you'll have in a matter of weeks." Bramwell knew it was time to go for the throat. He looked down at the twins. "Want to look at the badminton court and the pool?"

I was stunned. I was terrified that this was some bizarre fantasy that would *floof* away and leave me standing on a hill looking down at empty land. "Pool? Badminton court?"

Then I told myself that the badminton court would be a rectangle of dust, and the pool one of those plastic deals that fills halfway to your knees.

Nevertheless, I think my father knew that if he ended the negotiation now, before the twins and I *saw* that the pool and the badminton court were just makeshift, we might be a long time forgiving him.

He let Bramwell lead us out and around to the back of the house.

There was a badminton court. The asphalt was cracked here and there, but there were proper lines drawn on it, and a net that looked as if it could be mended. Behind the court was a metal post set on a tire with a tetherball attached, and to the left of that a tall wood post with a basketball hoop!

The twins were excited by the tetherball and basketball hoop, but it was the badminton court that got me. In all my life, I'd never known anybody who had a badminton court. *Sherman's* parents did not have a badminton court.

I was quite sure that not even the most popular girls in our school, not even Mike Harbinger, the most popular guy in *high* school, had their own badminton courts!

If the pool were no more than a wading tub, it didn't matter. A badminton court. Rich people in foreign movies had badminton courts. Badminton courts meant men in white flannel trousers and Irish hand-knit sweaters and white sneakers tossing racquets hand to hand easily, meant women with thin eyebrows and white sharkskin pleated skirts and perfectly enamelled fingernails, handsome people sitting around on lounge chairs drinking lemonade and talking about polo and art galleries.

From the badminton court, the north side of the lot rose, terraced, toward the street. Bramwell led us up steps carved out of the hill and filled with gravel held by railroad ties. So far I'd seen not a blade of grass, only bushes and trees, vines and ground covers, wild and intriguing.

On the first landing, the ruin of a gazebo stood all melancholy on a hexagonal gravel base.

This was altogether the most alluring and forsaken landscape I'd ever seen.

We followed Bramwell up another run of gravel

steps that angled away from the house, my father behind him, Sherman on my father's heels, the twins and me lagging to savor the yard. Ahead of us was a tall chain-link fence. Bramwell unhooked a padlock and pushed open the gate. We followed him onto a large, flat, flagstone terrace that surrounded a swimming pool—a genuine, sunken pool, a pool big enough to swim laps in, a pool with a *diving* board.

"Oh, gross," Sherman muttered.

The pool was empty, except for a coating of leaves and dirt and thick, smelly green slime.

I suppose a person could call it loathsome.

You think I was discouraged? "It could be cleaned, couldn't it?" I pictured that pool scrubbed, full of clear water on a summer day, with friends, hordes of friends, my friends, splashing around, sitting on beach towels spread across the flagstones. Even Mike Harbinger might visit a twelve-year-old if she had a swimming pool. I imagined the most popular girls in junior high lounging around my pool when Mike Harbinger and the high school stars he hung out with just happened to drop by.

I was looking at a whole lifestyle.

"So when do you want to move in?" Bramwell pressed the house keys into my father's hand.

We drove on downtown. I didn't dare push my father about the house. Suppose I only annoyed him enough to make him feel even more manipulated by Bramwell? If we lost this house I would remember, as an old, old woman, how I ruined my youth. Besides, there was Dow Jones to consider. After the heavy dues that dog had paid, of course the core of his life would be Bramwell. Even a week in a cage would be a return to hell for Dow Jones.

My father took Antony shopping, telling Sherman and me to meet them at the first floor's up escalator in an hour.

While Sherman bought a few presents, I managed to convince Aida that Antony did not need a tomb, and that stores did not generally stock them.

I was too bedazzled by that house to do any serious shopping myself.

A house with a swimming pool. Even before my mother left us to find herself, I don't think I ever imagined living in a house with a swimming pool.

When my father and brother met us, Antony was all excited, bursting with the strain of not telling Sherman and Aida and me what gifts he'd bought us.

Even driving home, none of us mentioned Bramwell's house. Views and badminton courts meant nothing to five-year-olds, and the empty pool, to them, was probably just a hole that couldn't even be dug in. Antony was far more interested in trying to convince Aida that what he really needed for Christmas was a tarantula.

Mrs. Farisee was home. The twins went right to the room they shared with me, I'm sure to show each other everything they'd bought.

Mrs. Farisee told Sherman to go home for lunch so that his family would not forget what he looked like.

After we ate, my father took her and the twins and me back to the house.

On the way there I was too thrilled to talk. Certainly he wouldn't go back unless he planned to take the place! Or maybe he just wanted to look at it again to convince himself it wasn't what he wanted. He didn't describe it to Mrs. Farisee. Maybe he didn't want to build it up too much . . . or make it seem too depressing.

Aida had other concerns. "If Santa gets stomach flu Christmas Eve, would he go home or just keep delivering presents?"

"What do you do if Santa throws up down your chimney?" Antony wondered.

But my sister had moved on to another thought. "Could we take Antony's trantular to the park if we promise it won't bite anybody?" she asked me.

The art of living with five-year-olds is in knowing when to tune them out.

As we pulled into the long gravel driveway, Mrs. Farisee was silent, impassive.

We stopped.

"Oh, my word," she pronounced as we got out of the car.

The minute my father led us into the living room, she made straight for the kitchen.

"There's a lot we could do with the place," he offered, almost apologetically.

She looked at the stained wallpaper and the filthy floor. "Like raze it."

Aida opened the door to the addition. "And here's . . ."

"I hope you're not planning to fit a human being in there," Mrs. Farisee said.

Sensing that our housekeeper was not pleased with the house, Aida didn't even offer to show her the bathroom in the garage.

My father led the way through the bedrooms. "We don't have a choice. I haven't found anybody who'll even *show* a house to a man with three children and three dogs."

I was so thrilled I found it hard not to yell. *We were going to take the place!*

Walking through the house, Mrs. Farisee was grim and silent. As my father ushered her out the back bedroom into the yard, she muttered, "Probably crawling with rattlesnakes in the summer."

Rattlesnakes.

Rattlesnakes had never entered my mind.

"It's better than being out on the streets, which is where we'll be if we don't take Bramwell's deal," my father pointed out.

"*Deal?*"

As my father explained about taking in Dow Jones, the twins went on reeling around the yard, giddy with the space and the wildness.

Rattlesnakes.

On the one hand, we had a view and a badminton court and a swimming pool.

I wasn't sure how all this stacked up against the possibility of rattlesnakes on our doorstep.

I didn't get to use the phone that evening. My father had a bunch of calls, and I had homework, and a lot on my mind.

3

"**R**attlesnakes," *I said.*

Sherman had come to walk with Antony and me to school Monday morning, as he always did. I waited until we were out of the house to bring up rattlesnakes, for fear Mrs. Farisee would tell me enough to convince me I didn't want the new house.

"What do you know about rattlesnakes?" I tend to use Sherman as an encyclopedia substitute.

"Why?" Sherman asked.

Without breaking stride, I pulled Antony's mittens off his ears, shoved his hands into the mittens, and put his cap back on his head. "Mrs. Farisee says the place Bramwell showed us will be crawling with them."

He looked at me in surprise. "Come on, Dez. There aren't any rattlesnakes in this part of the state. Besides, they stay away from people. And they hibernate all winter, anyway."

"Sherman, I'd feel better if you'd settle on just one solid answer." Still, he had relieved my mind.

"Dez, *people* my uncle might expose to rattlesnakes. But his dog, never."

"Hey, Antony!" It was Preston Harbinger, barreling down on us with a pod of kindergartners. Preston was about Antony's age, but shorter, with his black hair styled like some five-year-old executive's, and a wardrobe right out of *Gentleman's Quarterly*.

Mike Harbinger and his friends were about a quarter block behind, so we waited for them. Most of them were about sixteen, but they never put Sherman down. I think he was their Yoda, a cross between a mascot and a guru.

One thing about being a genius—sooner or later, somebody will respect you.

After we dropped off Mike and his gang at high school, and my brother and Preston at grade school, Sherman and I walked on to junior high.

Laurelle Carson was waiting out front for us.

Laurelle hung out with the most popular girls in junior high, but she'd turned out to be my best friend, next to Sherman.

"We found this wreck of a house," I told her, "but, boy, could it be neat!"

She was too excited to listen. "Guess what? Your dad asked my mom out! Isn't that terrific?"

I can't remember ever finding my father's social life terrific. While Mrs. Carson was a nice divorced woman, it seemed almost creepy to have my parent dating the parent of a friend of mine.

Elliot Lofting followed us into the building. Elliot is a person for whom the word *dour* was invented. He seems to disapprove of the world in general.

"Are you going to make any more vegetarian posters?" he asked.

"We're making some for Christmas." Sherman told him.

"Still saving turkeys," Elliot said.

Laurelle was ready to counter any sarcasm. "And pigs and cows and . . ."

"I got some great recipes for vegetarian Christmas dinners from People for the Ethical Treatment of Animals." Sherman was slow to notice sarcasm. "I'm going to attach copies to each poster so people can take them."

"Okay," Elliot blurted. "I can give you a hand.

Let me know when." He hurried away, as if embarrassed that he'd made a friendly overture, not to mention a moral commitment.

He didn't come near us at lunch, of course. Teena Brannigan and Kerri White and Marti Dunnigan and Laurelle always sat at the same table. An outsider would no more sit at that table than crash a White House breakfast. Of course, once Teena and the rest found out I knew Mike Harbinger, they started waving for me to join them. They even let Sherman come with me, because he was Mike's friend.

Still, only Laurelle and I said much to Sherman. His was an interesting situation. Because of him, Laurelle and I had become vegetarians. She had a lot of respect for him, but the others had yet to figure out how to take him. Here was this undersize wimp kid with a phenomenal IQ who hung out with the most important guys in high school.

His reflected glory didn't seem to affect Sherman's status with junior high boys, so maybe that's why he stuck with me and my new friends.

After lunch, Laurelle hung back with me. "Can you come over to my house after school?"

"I have to pick up Aida."

"That's okay. Bring her."

I knew she must really want me, if she was willing to have a five-year-old join us.

"Why don't you?" Sherman urged. "Elliot and I are going to be working on our vegetarian posters."

I didn't know how to refuse. I could hardly tell her that her mother dating my father made me uncomfortable.

Laurelle's street wasn't elegant like the Harbingers' or the Groves'. It was all tract houses, but they had two-car attached garages and front yards with trees and flowers.

I'd never been to her house before. The living room was sunny and tidy, full of plants, with white walls and a gold color carpet without a stain on it.

Laurelle's room was bigger than the one I shared with the twins. Her furniture was corny, a white four-poster bed with a white eyelet canopy and a white, gold-trimmed dresser. She even had a couple of old dolls on the top of a white bookcase.

I would have settled for that furniture, even if I had to have Storybook Dolls lined up on a shelf, just to have a room of my own.

Laurelle took the dolls off the shelves. "I loved these when I was little," she told Aida. "You want to play with them?"

Aida eyed them coolly. "You gots any mummies?"

Laurelle looked at me, confused.

"People do not keep mummies around the house," I told my sister firmly.

Laurelle looked concerned. "She means . . . real mummies? Like from Egypt?"

"It's just a phase," I said, trying to be offhand.

"So . . . ah . . . how about something to eat, Aida?" You have to hand it to Laurelle. How many twelve-year-olds would offer to feed a kindergartner who was interested only in mummies?

Mrs. Farisee kept our kitchen immaculate, but this one was not only clean, it had a built-in range and a big, new-looking refrigerator.

"You must like plants," I said. There were pots of chives and aloe in the kitchen.

"My mom's a florist. She just got her own shop."

It would be downright unsettling having my friend's mother married to my father, but Mrs. Carson, at least the one time I'd seen her, seemed to be a pleasant, gentle woman. And something could still fall through with Bramwell's house. Despite myself, I couldn't help imagining how we'd all share this Carson house. When you've been faced with living on the streets with your family and dogs, you tend to think a lot about shelter.

"You gots any Venus flytraps?" Aida inquired conversationally.

As we headed back to Laurelle's room, a door opened and her sister, Nicole, peered out. "I don't want you kids hogging the phone. I'm expecting a call."

Rattlesnakes again. As neat and clean and roomy as the house was, Laurelle's sister came with it.

She stomped in twice while we were listening to tapes and yelled at us to turn the volume down, then stormed in a third time to accuse Laurelle of trying on one of her sweaters.

No. The house we lived in now had two bedrooms and one bathroom and five people, but it would feel less crowded than sharing the Carsons', no matter how many bedrooms and bathrooms.

No matter how well I got along with Laurelle, her house would always feel like Carson territory.

And it had no swimming pool.

Whatever it took, I had to see that we accepted Bramwell's deal.

My father didn't get home until just before dinner. He looked tired, so I decided I'd wait until after dessert to bring up the house.

While he was passing the peas, he announced, "I talked to Bramwell Grove. We're taking the place." He glanced at the tower of mashed potatoes my brother had constructed. "Antony, you do not spread strawberry jam on potatoes."

"It's guava." Antony hesitated, a spoonful of jam over the potato peak. "This is a volcano and it's ready to be cupped and the jam is the guava."

I sat there with my mouth full of peas, so relieved about the house that I got tears in my eyes.

"Not be cupped," my father said. "Erupt."

I was so thrilled I almost leaned over to hug him.

"What would Santa do," Antony asked nobody in particular, "if he was flying over a volcano just as it be . . . just as it blew up?"

"If you're planning to use your spoon as a catapult for those peas in it," Mrs. Farisee warned Aida, "put the idea out of your head."

"You can all stay at the same schools," my father told the twins and me. "I checked with the district office. Since you'll have to take a bus, they'll even switch Aida to morning kindergarten with Antony." He passed the bread to Mrs. Farisee. "So they'll be coming home on the bus together at noon."

"I won't be there. I'll see you moved, but I'm not coming with you."

It was almost as if my *father* announced he wasn't going to live with us anymore. He stared at her, as shocked as I.

"I'm not going to be stuck in the wilderness at my age," she declared.

"But it's only a few miles to downtown," my father said.

"With no city bus service. Driving up that hill

and turning into that driveway, you're taking your life in your hands. Not to mention rattlesnakes."

"Oh, rattlesnakes." I hurried to set her straight. "Sherman says there aren't any in this part of the state. Also, rattlesnakes stay away from people. And they hibernate all winter."

"Sherman," she snorted, as if I'd cited Geraldo Rivera as an authority.

"But we *need* you!" I blurted.

"Antony," she snapped, "get your hand out of the gravy."

"See?" I challenged. "Already he's regressing."

"No," he said. "I'm wading. The gravy is the guava and my fingers are the people trapped in guava."

"Lava," my father told him absently. "Mrs. Farisee, if it's a matter of money . . ."

"It's not a matter of anything. I'm giving notice here and now. I'm moving in with my sister. Her kids are running her ragged. What they need in that house is order."

That, I knew, Mrs. Farisee would bring to her sister's home and family. Nevertheless, I felt as if I were standing on the edge of a cliff that was being washed away by the waves below, or by a flow of guava. "We need you more!" I protested.

"Blood," she announced, "is thicker than water."

This got the twins' attention. "How thick . . ." Aida began.

"Never mind," I said.

I knew that the idea Mrs. Farisee might really leave us would take a long time to penetrate the defenses the twins had learned. When our mother explained to us that she was going away for a while to find herself, they seemed barely to listen. It was days after she actually left before they began to grieve.

When we finished dinner, my father said to the twins and me, "You go on to your room. I'll help Mrs. Farisee tidy up."

He had never helped her with the dishes before.

From our room, I could hear the two of them talking, their voices low and civilized. I tried to do my homework, but all I could do was listen, even though I couldn't make out the words.

I waited for ten minutes after the voices stopped.

My father was sitting at the dining room table, writing a lot of figures on a pad. "It's going to cost to move, but we can swing it."

"She's not leaving because of a fourth dog, is she?"

"It's not the dog, Dez. She doesn't want to move to our new place."

"Did you . . ."

"Honey, do you think anybody in the world could

change Mrs. Farisee's mind once she made it up?"

I went to bed, reflecting that I would have felt better if I'd never had the talk with him. It was hard getting to sleep, thinking, as I did when my mother left, that maybe it was because of us, maybe we were too much for any woman to put up with.

Mrs. Farisee was true to her word. She helped us pack. I kept thinking that somehow one of us could convince her to stay. I couldn't bring myself to ask her, because I was half afraid she'd admit that she just didn't want to be with us anymore. Besides, I knew that if I tried to talk to her about staying, she'd cut me off with, "The matter is closed."

The packing got to the twins. They followed Mrs. Farisee around, big-eyed, not daring to cling to her, but not wanting her out of their sight.

With all our frantic packing and cleaning, my father still managed to see Ruth Carson Tuesday evening. I couldn't help thinking that the least he could do was stay home with his kids, who were going through loss and trauma.

Wednesday evening, after Mrs. Farisee and the twins had gone to bed, I went into the parlor to talk to him.

It's funny how, in the most terrible situations, your mind will seize on one small thing. Maybe that's because it's all you can handle.

"What are we going to do for Christmas?" I asked.

"We'll have Christmas. Christmas will not be stricken from the calendar." Then he took pity on me. "We'll do something."

"Aunt and the captain will be back from their honeymoon. Maybe they'll invite us for Christmas dinner."

Aunt wasn't our real aunt, but for years my parents thought she must be a relative because she'd brought a present to their wedding, and visited us every few summers. It turned out she just liked to go to weddings and visit strangers.

When she stayed with us a few months earlier, she'd met Langley Morris, a retired sea captain who, as my father put it, took her off our hands. My father was a good man, but now and then he had a streak of humor I didn't like.

Still, I couldn't stop talking my uneasiness out. "It's December ninth already. Maybe we should invite them."

"Dez, we'll be in no shape to have company for a holiday dinner just days after we move."

"If we invite them, maybe it'll nudge them into asking us." I knew I was talking around what was bothering me."

I think he was relieved to be faced with a minor problem for a change. "What if we ask them and they accept? We'd have to take them to a restaurant, which is probably the last place they'd want to go. And do you realize what it would cost?"

I didn't have the energy to follow up the argument, or to hold off the awful, heavy despair. "Yeah. The main thing is, how are we going to live without Mrs. Farisee?"

He put an arm around me and rested his chin on my hair.

"At least Sherman's right about rattlesnakes," I murmured. "Bramwell would never risk his dog getting bitten."

But then it occurred to me that he would be leaving Dow Jones with us in December, when snakes hibernate.

Laurelle was waiting at my locker Wednesday morning. "Guess what? My mom won a weekend ski trip—she sold more FTDs or something."

"FTDs?" Teena looked impressed. "Your mother sells sports cars?"

"My mother," Laurelle told her patiently, "is a florist. FTD means flowers by delivery." She turned back to me. "Anyway, she was going to give the trip to somebody, since she'd broken up with her boyfriend, but now she's asked your dad to go. I mean,

she must really like him, because she can't even ski."
She looked concerned suddenly. "Oh, *guy*! I just
hope she doesn't make a fool of herself or break some
gross bone or something."

There is not much that prepares you for one of
your best friends announcing that her mother is
going away for a weekend with your father. I couldn't
just stand there looking thunderstruck. "When is it?"

"The weekend of the eighteenth."

I couldn't help feeling sorry for her, and relieved
for myself. What kind of mother would leave her
kids a week before Christmas? "Then it's out, Laurelle. We're moving on the thirteenth."

"I know. But that's five days before they go."

How did she know what day we were moving?
Had I told her? "My father would never go away and
leave us that close to Christmas."

"It is a week before Christmas," she said firmly,
"and five days after you move."

No, I told myself. No father would leave his kids
just five days after uprooting them. Never.

I didn't feel like standing around arguing with
her. "I have to go up to the library," I told Sherman.

I barely had time to look up rattlesnakes before
the bell rang. There were months to go before the
end of hibernation, I told myself.

Walking to class, I decided that however certain Laurelle seemed, she had to be wrong. She must have had some father, to think that mine would go away with her mother and leave us in a new house a week before Christmas.

At lunchtime, I went on down to the infirmary. "Could I lie down in here?"

"What's the matter?" Ms. Dettweiler, our school nurse, was square-built and grizzled and about as fluttery as a pit bull.

"My brain cells are rebelling, and I am too disgusted with life in general to contend with the human race at lunch."

"Sounds logical to me." Ms. Dettweiler led me behind the curtain to where the cots were and turned down the blanket on the closest one. "Everybody has a day like that now and then."

I sat on the cot and took off my shoes. "Ms. Dettweiler, I have a *life* like that."

"Eat your lunch. I don't want you coming back here with dizzy spells. And don't you dare get crumbs on the bed."

I'd finished eating when I heard a voice in the front of the infirmary—Laurelle's. "Ms. Dettweiler, have you seen Desdemona Blank? I can't find her anywhere."

"She's resting," Ms. Dettweiler said.

"Oh, boy. What is it? Is she going to be all right?"

"She just needs to be quiet, okay? She'll be going to classes, so don't worry, and don't harass her."

When I heard the bell ring for class, I put on my shoes, thanked Ms. Dettweiler, and left the infirmary.

Laurelle was waiting in the hall. Plainly, she and Ms. Dettweiler had different ideas of harassment.

Looking worried, Laurelle fell into step beside me. "Are you okay? Did you faint or something? Did you have your period? Ms. Dettweiler has some pamphlets . . ."

You can't tell a friend who worries about you to bug off. "I was just . . . I needed a rest."

"Yeah. I guess moving and all. But you should still probably have a checkup."

At the beginning of the year the idea of Laurelle Carson even noticing me seemed too much to hope for. Now she was shadowing me, even overseeing my health.

Concerned she was, but not dense. "You're not mad about my mother asking your dad on the trip, are you?"

"No." I was certainly not mad about it.

We walked on toward my class, and then, without

even knowing I was going to, I asked, "Don't you feel funny at all about your mother going away with a man for a weekend?"

She flushed. "Oh, come on, Dez! It's a ski trip, not some kind of assig . . . assig . . ."

Sherman caught up with us. "Assignation? Rendezvous? Tryst? Romantic interlude?"

Hearing it, I was embarrassed myself. "I didn't mean that," I told Laurelle. "I just mean . . ."

She stopped, not even asking Sherman how much he'd heard, not even caring how much more he heard. "Look. In one week my mom's boyfriend dumped her and my father told her he's marrying somebody half her age. I thought she might never take an interest in herself again."

"How can you be sure my father won't dump her?" After all, I knew the man's record.

"She either takes that chance or mopes around crying. Besides, your father is a psychologist. They have rules about how they treat people."

"Ethics," Sherman said.

She nodded. "Yeah. Rules about not wrecking people's lives."

I didn't have the heart to tell her that the rules applied only to on-the-job relationships.

At the door of my class, she asked, "You want to

come over after school? My mom could drive you home."

I wasn't even tempted. "We have to take some cleaning stuff up to the new house."

Mrs. Farisee had already packed up our summer clothes, sealing them in cardboard cartons commandeered from every store she went to. When I got home, she put me to work with the twins packing up books and toys I knew we'd want before we moved.

She had dinner on the table minutes after my father walked in, then sent him and me up to the new house with cartons of scouring powder and sprays and rags while she packed away the dishes and pans she wouldn't be using in the next few days.

The heat and electricity hadn't been turned on at Bramwell's house. My father muttered about utility companies that didn't follow through on their promises. I had planned to stake a claim on the back bedroom, with its glass wall, but I realized this was not the best time for negotiating.

Since it was too dark to do any real cleaning, all we could do was leave the supplies and drive home.

There was no reason to expect him to tell me about Ruth Carson's invitation. I had no business asking about his private life. I knew Laurelle was wrong.

He would never go away on a pleasure trip a week before Christmas. But I was curious as to just how serious his dating her mother was getting. "So Mrs. Carson asked you on a ski trip?"

He didn't take his eyes off the road. "Weekend of the eighteenth."

"That's a dumb time to ask anybody with kids to go away."

"You'll be fine," he said.

I wasn't sure he meant what he seemed to mean. "But you're not going."

"I just told you. Weekend of the eighteenth."

I was so shocked I could feel tears in my eyes. "You're going to dump all the moving on us while you go skiing with some *woman?*"

"We'll be all moved in and settled by then. And, believe me, by then I'll need the relaxation."

"What about Christmas shopping?" I could hear my voice getting a little too high. "What about a Christmas tree?"

He was calm. "We can take care of all that when I get back. We'll get a live tree and plant it . . ."

I had known this man all my life. I had trusted him. It was as if he'd suddenly been inhabited by some icy, remorseless alien being. I didn't even feel related to him at the moment. "So you leave your three kids alone practically in the wilderness while you *relax*?"

He was patient. Of course, if you have no human feelings, it's not difficult to be patient. "Dez, it's hardly wilderness, and you'll have three big dogs, plus Laurelle and Nicole."

Nicole. Had it been The Terminator II sitting there beside me, I would still not have expected this. "*Nicole? Nicole Carson?*"

His voice got lower, and his words more deliberate. "She is a perfectly responsible girl, and her mother trusts her completely."

"The Germans trusted Hitler. Why don't you just call up some maximum security prison and ask them to send us somebody out of solitary?"

He turned up the heater. "Don't try to break me down with drama. It's all settled."

"You are abandoning your own children up in the hills with some girl whose blood could freeze a tropical rain forest?"

Not even a psychologist can endure his own children indefinitely without reacting. "That's enough," he warned.

As soon as we pulled up in front of our house, I scrambled out of the car. "*And what kind of a father moves his own kids into a place that's crawling with rattlesnakes anyway?*"

He didn't even come in, just drove away and left me.

Mrs. Farisee was stacking up books in the parlor. "Get much done?" she greeted me.

"If Laurelle Carson calls, would you tell her I'm busy?"

Thursday morning, I told Sherman, "I don't want to get to school until the last minute."

"Sure." He slowed down. "Why?"

"Why?" Antony echoed.

"Can't a person have a private reason?" I demanded. "Is it against the law or something?"

I managed to get to school late enough to miss Laurelle. But I knew I couldn't hide out in the infirmary every lunch hour. I knew, too, that after the scene with my father, I'd better not try to get sent home claiming to be sick. Besides, being home with Mrs. Farisee would just remind me that in a few days she'd be out of our lives forever. *What kind of father goes off and leaves kids who've just lost their housekeeper?*

I knew I'd look odd eating alone outside, so I went down to the lunchroom at noon.

Laurelle was waiting for me with Sherman. "Guess what?"

"I know," I said.

"Know what?" Sherman asked.

"I can't wait," she burbled. "I'm dying to see your new house, and your pool! I'll bring a bunch of tapes. Do you have a microwave? I'll bring some popcorn that has only half the calories of the other kinds."

Here she was, my *friend*, all excited at spending the weekend at my house. As a matter of fact, I would have been looking forward as much as she was to having her stay over, if my father weren't going away with her mother, and if Nicole weren't coming. Before I became The Girl Who Knows Mike Harbinger, I would have been surprised if somebody as popular as Laurelle Carson even talked to me.

If only she and I could have been kids with old-fashioned two-parent families.

"So tomorrow morning we're coming to help you move," she announced.

No! I thought. Nobody else who sees the filthy rooms and tattered draperies will understand what a great house it can be. I don't want anybody else looking at the pool until it's clean and full. Besides, how did things get so heavy between my father and Ruth Carson so fast? Dating is one thing. Even going away for a *tryst* is one thing. But wrestling desks and cartons around together suggests a real commitment.

Maybe a blizzard will come up just for tomorrow morning, I told myself. And with any luck, another storm will hit next Friday, with travel alerts, and nobody able to do anything but stay home.

4

At dinner, I realized that I couldn't spend the years until I was eighteen and on my own without speaking directly to my father. "What happens to the twins after school from now on, with nobody home afternoons?" I couldn't help glancing at Mrs. Farisee, thinking surely this would move her to relent.

My father spoke as if he and I had been communicating comfortably all along. "I'll pick them up from school on my lunch hour and take them to a day-care center."

How could Mrs. Farisee keep the concrete around her heart from cracking?

Silently, she cut the pineapple upside-down cake she'd baked us.

She had cartons and cartons of stuff packed for us to take up to the new house after dinner.

At six the next morning, Ruth Carson and Laurelle showed up to help us finish packing. Of course, Nicole didn't come. Nicole, I was sure, wouldn't risk chipping a fingernail even to save the planet from the greenhouse effect.

Mrs. Carson wasn't big, but she was strong. She and Laurelle worked as hard as any of us loading the car.

My father left the twins with Mrs. Farisee while we four drove up to the new house.

I must confess, Laurelle and her mother had a lot of class. Neither mentioned the state the place was in. Ruth said the view was glorious, and the parlor enormous. Laurelle said the fireplace was fabulous.

I was braced for them to ask to see the pool.

Then the scary thing happened. Ruth whispered to Laurelle, who went outside, and came in carrying what looked like a detecting device from a sci-fi movie, mounted on a pole.

"It's solar." Laurelle thrust it at me. "For your pool. It doesn't use any electricity, just turns on at twilight."

"Oh . . ." My father was plainly touched. He thanked Laurelle and gave Ruth a *look*, as if he'd hug her or something if the rest of us weren't there.

Of course, he took the thing right up and installed it on the path just before the pool area.

Again, Laurelle and her mother had to be classy. Cruddy and smelly and disgusting as the pool was, both went on about how wonderful it would be come summer.

We got back to our house at eight. Laurelle and her mother left, Ruth to open her shop, Laurelle to clean her room. If my father hadn't been involved with Mrs. Carson, I would have thought about what good people they were.

The moving van was about to leave.

Mrs. Farisee had the house all cleaned, and her suitcases in the empty parlor.

When her taxi came, the driver and my father loaded her luggage in the trunk. I really believed that she'd relent at the last moment and stay.

She picked up her carry-on bag, then set it down and hugged me, then the twins, and shook hands with my father.

She stepped into the taxi. And she was gone.

Of course there wasn't time for us to drive her to the airport and come back for the dogs and meet the movers at the new house. I knew that. Still, it seemed so cold to let her go alone.

She was out of sight before Antony and Aida screamed. It was like one shared cry, one long, heartbroken wail. They started to run after the cab, but my father and I grabbed them.

"I will never lose anybody again, ever," I muttered to him.

The dogs were nervous and uneasy. Humans generally maintain that animals don't feel things as we do, partly because people don't stop to pay the right kind of attention, partly because not admitting the feelings of beasts makes it more acceptable to abuse them.

My brother and sister kept crying in the car, dry, choking sobs, the kind that make a little kid vomit if it goes on long.

Shivering, whining softly, the dogs kept licking the twins' faces, and the twins clung to them, getting their fur all soggy.

When we picked up Chinese fast-food take-out, the dogs didn't even try to free themselves and snuffle at the cartons.

It's amazing how losing one person can screw up a whole family, even to the beasts.

When we got to our new house, the moving van was pulling into the driveway. I took the twins and the dogs out to the fenced service yard. Too old to huddle with them in a soggy lump, I sat close, feeling dried out and sick.

The movers were finished in an hour or so. Our family was not heavy on belongings.

When my father called us for dinner, the dogs followed us into the kitchen. When he put them out into the service yard again, they sat leaning against the door.

It doesn't do kids or dogs any good to be transplanted time after time. We get root shock.

My father and I moved the food around on our plates, but the twins were too demoralized to abuse their food.

Nobody even looked at the fortunes in the cookies.

My father put the cartons in the refrigerator. "I've advertised for a new housekeeper, but we can't figure on anybody starting until after the holidays."

After dinner, Laurelle called. "My mom says with your moving into a new house and all, you'll have a mess on your hands. She's going to invite you all over for Christmas dinner!"

I wasn't sure how I felt. Certainly, if Langley Morris and Aunt didn't invite us, we faced a depressing meal in a restaurant, which would probably be a hassle, with me being vegetarian. Since Laurelle was one, too, at least her mother would serve a main dish other than turkey. On the other hand, Ruth Carson was getting so close so fast it was hard for me to remember that once I worried that my father would never settle down.

Now that we had a house with three bedrooms and a pool, we didn't need anybody coming into our lives.

Except a housekeeper.

It wasn't until bedtime that I truly realized that I had my own room at last, and the one I'd coveted, the back bedroom with the glass wall. Before I knew Mrs. Farisee was leaving, I'd imagined that having any kind of room of my own would be all I'd need to make me happy.

I was hanging up clothes in my closet, my own, unshared closet, when my father came in carrying two cups of hot chocolate. "You want to talk?"

I didn't, really, but you can hardly leave your own father standing in the doorway with a steaming mug in each hand.

Why did he always think food or drink would help? I wondered. Was it something prehistoric, going back to the days when mammoths were scarce and starvation always around the corner? Or maybe sometimes parents simply have no other comfort to offer.

We went out to the living room and sat on the old ruptured Hide-A-Bed. I realized that he wouldn't have to sleep on it, or in the parlor, anymore. But I would have traded all the space and privacy, even my own room, to have Mrs. Farisee back.

And, sitting with him now, I couldn't ignore the other thing. I looked down into the steam. "I suppose you're still going away?"

He nodded. "Friday."

"And leaving us with Nicole."

"Mmm-hmm. We'll be back Sunday evening."

I wanted to say *I wish we'd never met Ruth Carson or found this house*, but I knew that would be infantile, and maybe only half true. After all, even losing Mrs. Farisee beat being out on the street with no place to live.

"I know you hate my going." He took a sip of chocolate. "But I'm not even tempted to call it off in order to have peace at home. If you let your kids start running your life, you're all lost." He could say the hardest things in the nicest voice.

"You could at least have some consideration."

"That is one of the biggest guilt-maker lines people can lay on other people. It ranks right up there with 'If you really loved me . . .' "

"Okay." I was too tired and empty to endure one

of his intellectual arguments. "I just don't know why you have to go away when . . ."

"When what?"

"When everybody else is leaving me." I had no idea this was what I was thinking until I heard myself say it. Then, even though I wasn't reconciled with my father, I went on spilling my feelings. "Mrs. Farisee just leaves as if we meant nothing at all to her. All year I've walked Antony to school and Aida home, and now I'll be taking some bus with them, a bus full of people I probably don't even know. I don't know whether I should sit with the twins, or what everybody will think if I do. Even Sherman . . . Sherman is my best friend in the world, and now we won't ever walk to school or home together. And in the middle of everything, my own father just takes off. I feel as if I'm standing on a curb in the middle of the night in a scary part of a strange big city watching everybody I care about walk away. I try to call to them, but I can't make a sound, and nobody even looks back."

"Oh, honey." He set down his cup and held me, breathing all over the top of my head. At least he had the grace not to remind me there'd been a time when I would have given anything to *lose* Sherman, a wimp kid who trailed me everywhere.

"And I'll be coming home to an empty house."

He stroked my hair. "I wish I could say that you never really lose anybody you care about, but that's not true. People change, and they move, and some you lose. You and the twins will leave me some day. But you never lose all your family—unless, of course, you can't stand anybody in it. You won't be coming home to an empty house. Until we get a new housekeeper, you can walk home with Laurelle and I'll pick you up after I get the twins."

You don't pull away from your father when he thinks he's comforting you, but I lifted my head. "Have you asked her mother?"

"It was Ruth's idea."

There was no sense piling a new fight on everything I had to contend with.

I went to my room less comforted than I'd been before the hot chocolate and the talk.

Don't think about it, I told myself, not even bothering to close the tattered draperies over the window wall. Don't think about anything but being in your own room, in a house with a badminton court and a swimming pool. When you first saw the place you were crazy to live here.

Outside, the wind was tormenting the trees.

Through the chill winter dark, I could see the lights below, lights that seemed to go on forever, house lights, colored neon lights, and the flowing ribbons of car lights. I remember one of the first dreams I had, when I was too young to tell anybody about it. I was sitting on a hill, looking down at tiny, tiny people, driving by in tiny, tiny cars. I was close enough to touch them, but they went about their business, either ignoring me or not even knowing I was there. The lights now were as wonderful, as mysterious as that dream. Maybe another time I would have felt the magic of standing at my own window, watching the night's life. But all I felt was alone and disconnected, with the people, their lights, and their lives so far from me, knowing nothing about me, caring not at all.

I turned out my lamp, but I couldn't sleep. This is your own private room, I told myself. Appreciate it, dummy!

The wind got rougher, and I could hear branches scratch the walls outside like lost cats desperate to come in.

I heard footsteps in the hall, then in my room.

Without a word, my brother and sister climbed into my bed.

Click . . . click . . . click.

Dog nails on the floor.

Thunk . . . thunk . . . thunk.

Very deliberately, very slowly, one leg at a time, Herb and Joe and Sadie climbed onto the bed.

They circled and turned and worried the covers and pawed the blankets and finally settled down.

I lay hemmed in, not able to move, kids at my chest and my back, dogs draped over my legs. At least, I thought, there are six of us I can count on to stick together.

We spent the weekend putting things away, eating cereal for breakfast, driving into town for take-out food or quick meals.

Monday, my father drove us all to school. We passed Preston and his friends, and Sherman with Mike and his gang.

Neither the twins nor I had the spirit to ask my father to let us out.

Laurelle and Sherman were waiting at my locker.

"How about we put up some of our vegetarian fliers Wednesday after school?" he greeted me. "Then we can put up the rest next Monday when we see how many have been torn down."

At any other time I would have been eager to see the fliers.

I nodded.

"So that's settled." Laurelle turned her attention to me. "We're going to have such a neat time this weekend. It's just too bad Nicole has to come."

"Nicole?" Sherman sounded as if he'd inhaled part of the Sahara.

"She is so teed off that we have to stay with you," Laurelle went on. "She accused my mom of forcing her into involuntary baby-sitting. Also, my mom told her she couldn't have company up there, which your father probably wouldn't allow anyway. On top of that, Nicole's to do no driving except in an emergency, since you're on such a winding road. She says no mother has the right to take a whole weekend out of her daughter's life while she goes away with some guy she hardly knows. I'm telling you, it got pretty hairy."

"Your sister is going to spend the weekend at Dez's house?" Sherman rasped.

How does this kid get the habit of falling in love with older women? I wondered, walking to class flanked by him and Laurelle. Is it in his genes, or just part of his general oddness? Maybe it's a stage all boys go through. At least this time it wasn't one of my *father's* women.

I suppose I was feeling especially put out with

Sherman because I couldn't help seeing that Nicole's fussing was not so different from my own.

I never thought the day would come when I would defend Nicole Carson. "Most people probably get uneasy about their parents getting in too deep with some guy too fast, Laurelle. For all you know, my father could be a real jerk."

"Nah." Laurelle was not to be shaken. Then she got more serious. "Listen, he's my mother's generation, not some young stud. He has a regular job. So far he hasn't phoned her from a tanning salon or tried to borrow her car or her earrings. He's the best thing that's come along since my father split on us."

She was still upbeat at lunch. "You ought to see Dez's new house!" she announced to everybody at the table. "It's got the greatest fireplace!"

Teena and Kerri and Marti went on talking. Now that I've moved, I thought, they don't see me walking to school with Mike and his friends. I'm just me again, not The Girl Who Knows Mike Harbinger. What if some day Sherman and I sit at this table and nobody but Laurelle talks to me?

"Also a badminton court and a swimming pool," I said casually. After all, nobody was going to see either before summer.

"A huge swimming pool, and in the ground, not

some plastic deal," Laurelle added.

It's amazing, and pretty disillusioning, some of the things people respect you for. Right away, I was the center of attention.

"A swimming pool?" Teena asked. "Does Mike Harbinger know you have a swimming pool?"

Now that I had a reaction, I was casual. "I don't know. My brother Antony has probably told Mike's little brother. They're best friends."

"*Wow.*" Kerri sat back, absorbing all the implications. "Dez, come summer, we can have pool parties! Maybe even Mike and his friends will come!"

"Yeah," Marti breathed. "I'll just have to lose five pounds by June."

After school, they all walked Laurelle and me to her house, asking how big the pool was, how deep, whether it was heated, and whether I was planning to ask Mike to drop by and see it soon.

I couldn't help feeling that my social standing depended on having a hot summer.

"I heard Mike's on the swim team," Teena said.

They all looked at me as if I were the authority on Mike Harbinger's activities.

It was odd. A few months earlier, I had such a crush on him I couldn't even say his name. But then we were thrown together. We had to shepherd Antony and Aida and Preston through a museum. We got drafted to work at a party Sherman's parents gave, a party where I accidentally fed Jake truffles and the guests dog food. We ducknapped a pair of fowl doomed to be a Grove family banquet.

Maybe at twelve, dog food canapes and duck manure tend to quell romantic feelings. Or, more likely, I had enough sense to realize that there's a big difference between twelve and sixteen.

Besides, he'd turned out to be such a good friend, it would have ruined everything if I kept *yearning* after him.

"He is so gorgeous," Kerri sighed. "How can you stand it?"

"I bet he's a great swimmer, too," Teena mused. "I've got to take lessons."

I was tempted to remind them that it wasn't even Christmas yet, but you don't fritter away your social status with sensible statements.

When they finally left, Laurelle got out her family photo albums, which made me a little uneasy, as if she were introducing me to all her relatives in advance.

I was relieved when I heard a horn outside, and looked out to see our car.

Laurelle walked me to the curb.

"We'll stop at the hardware store for paint and then grab something to eat," my father greeted me.

"Bramwell is bringing Dow Jones up."

It was not a mere hardware store he took us to but a store that sold safe and environmentally sound products.

Antony and Aida, without even conferring, picked out a brick red enamel for their walls.

"You get white, off-white, blue, or beige flat-coat," my father said.

The twins looked at each other.

Antony started to unzip his parka.

"If you don't cut a deal with your father," I told him, "we may not get out of here in time, and Bramwell Grove won't leave us his dog."

Little kids never have too many dogs.

I had decided my room should have pale violet walls, and a dark purple deep-pile shag rug, just to offset any creeping Laurelle-itis.

"It's going to be a long time before we can afford any rugs," my father said.

I could have pointed out that a man who couldn't afford rugs should not be blowing his money on ski trips, but I didn't. There was no sense making a fuss when your parent was about to give you your choice of wall colors. Especially when he was paying forty dollars a gallon for paint that didn't give off noxious fumes.

At dinner, I couldn't help thinking with some wistfulness of the days when I thought fast-food restaurants were a treat. It seemed to me that even a simple meal, cooked at home and eaten in our own kitchen, would be a relief. Besides, not many fast-food places cater to vegetarians.

As we pulled into the driveway of our new house, our dogs, inside, began howling and barking in greeting.

I wasn't too worried about how my dogs would greet Dow Jones. As my father had pointed out, they were all neutered. Since about one out of every ten puppies and kittens born in this country finds a home, and the rest either starve slowly or are killed less painfully at a pound, I have no respect for people who don't have their dogs and cats neutered. Neutered cats and dogs are healthier and happier. The males lose the dumb urge to fight with other males. As for the females, I've often wondered how human women would feel if they had half a dozen babies at once, loved and nursed them, only to have them all taken away forever at a few weeks old.

As Nicholas Cage said in *Raising Arizona*, "It's a hard world for small things."

Before we had a chance to get out of our car,

Bramwell came roaring up in his blue Maserati.

"Okay." Except for going away and leaving his kids without a qualm, my father is a compassionate, sensible man. "We have to make this easy on him."

I assumed he meant the dog.

"You," I told the twins, "stay where you are."

I knew that if we let them come in with us, they would surely do something that would let our three dogs come tumbling out to that unscratched, fresh-waxed Maserati.

My father lifted a hand to Bramwell, half greeting, half warning, then unlocked our front door.

Roaring "Sit! Back! Down!" at Herb and Sadie, holding them back with a foot, he leashed Joe. He handed me the lead, and blocked Herb and Sadie with his leg while Joe dragged me outside. Then he backed out and slammed the door, leaving Herb and Sadie to howl.

Under the porch light, he already looked like a man who'd run an obstacle race.

He took the lead from me. "Joe, stay!"

Bramwell climbed out, carrying Dow Jones, leaving the car's headlights on. I could not help but wonder if he wanted to be ready for a quick escape.

Dow Jones did not resist. Dow Jones shut his eyes and went catatonic.

Aida scrambled out of the car, Antony beside her. "Did he die?" my sister wondered. "Will we have to mum . . ."

My father put a hand on Aida's shoulder. "If either of you *moves*, if either of you *speaks*, you will regret it for the rest of your days."

His voice was so terrible they both froze.

Being five, of course, they had only a dim idea of the rest of their lives.

I was very uneasy about the impression we were making on Bramwell. Would he leave his dog with a psychologist who threatened his own children? If Dow Jones didn't stay, would the deal be off? Could I endure being reevicted, this time from a house with my own violet-walled room, a house with a badminton court and a swimming pool?

"Put your dog down," my father advised Bramwell. "We have to give them a chance to get acquainted."

Dow Jones scrambled desperately up Bramwell, so that his front legs were on the man's shoulders.

"Poor dog. Poor baby," Aida crooned.

"How many days is our rest of our lifes?" Antony asked my father.

"Do we have to not move for how many days we have the rest of?" Aida wondered.

73

Carefully, Bramwell set his dog down on the driveway.

Joe lunged toward Dow Jones, tail waving frantically, with my father hauling on the leash, yelling "Stay!"

Dow Jones tried to scramble back into the car, but Bramwell snatched him up.

"They are going to get in a horrible battle," Aida declared dolefully.

"Quiet!" my father growled. "Grove, if you don't put your dog down . . ."

"I know. I know." Bramwell set Dow Jones on the gravel again and squatted beside him, his hand on the dog's neck.

As Joe hauled my father toward them, I saw Bramwell's hand tremble.

Little by little, my father let Joe scrabble toward them.

In the glare of the headlights, I saw a tiny muscle under Bramwell's left eye twitch, but he held his dog still.

A couple of feet from them, Joe flattened his forelegs on the pavement, his hind legs straight, his rear up in the air, his tail wagging so fast it was a blur. He whined. He laid the side of his muzzle on the drive, tongue lolling.

Dow Jones looked away, as if embarrassed by the spectacle.

"We should have a turnip kit ready in case they have a horrible battle and one of them gets all torn up." My brother was somber.

"*Grab them apart!*" Aida wailed.

"You do not make another sound!" my father said through his teeth.

"So we put the turnip kit on the leg or whatever gets broken and twist a stick through it to stop the blood." Antony made a token compliance by lowering his voice. "But you gots to loosen the turnip kit every five minutes or the legs gets fang green."

"*Twist a stick through their legs?*" Aida's cry drowned out the howling from the house.

"Nobody is going to need a tourniquet, and nobody is getting gangrene, and if you say another word I will toss your television into a gully!" my father roared.

I bet he never talked to his clients that way.

Nevertheless, it worked. Antony gasped and moved close to Aida, who grabbed his hand.

I could not help thinking what an impression we must be making on our new landlord.

My father let Joe scrunch closer to Bramwell and

his dog. Grinning, Joe reached up to bat the other dog's grizzled muzzle.

Dow Jones's tail barely flicked.

Rear end wagging, Joe swatted him gently across the nose again.

Dow Jones's tail moved faster.

My father and Bramwell led them back into the enclosed yard, Joe veering to shoulder Dow Jones at almost every step.

"It's going to be fine," my father assured our landlord. "Only two more dogs to go."

5

When Sherman and I sat down at the cafeteria table Tuesday, everybody stopped talking.

You can't help but feel paranoid when people shut up the minute you're near enough to hear them.

Then Kerri White announced, as if an idea had suddenly occurred to her, "I was just thinking. We ought to give Dez a housewarming. We could invite Mike Harbinger and some of his friends, since she knows them."

Teena, Marti, and Laurelle looked as if they'd each been offered a free make-over right out of the blue.

"Wow! Yes!"

"What a great idea!"

"When?"

Sherman didn't say anything, but he seldom did in front of this bunch.

Had it not been for the talk of inviting Mike, I might have been more touched. Still, who's going to discourage her friends from throwing her a party? In my whole life nobody but my parents had ever had a party for me.

"Maybe right after Christmas," Laurelle said.

They went on talking about the party. Teena said it should have a theme, but Kerri and Marti told her nobody under forty had a *theme* for a party, unless it was in old movies about 1950 high school proms.

From the arguing, it was clear that they hadn't plotted it down to the details.

Kerri and Marti and Teena stayed after school, since Faye Brower had promised to bring her sister's batons and show them some twirling. Laurelle and I walked to her house alone. Sherman tagged along for a few blocks, but he chickened out at the last minute and went on home.

For a while, it looked as if it would be all right. Nicole wasn't there. Laurelle made no move to drag out more family albums.

Instead, she showed me the new clothes her mother had bought for the ski trip.

My father had never owned ski clothes, so far as I knew.

After he picked me up, he took the twins and me to a pizza place. While I walked along the salad bar, I wondered what he was going to wear skiing. Surely the man had more brains than to buy new clothes for one weekend.

If he bought ski clothes it would mean that

    A.   His brains had run out his ears.

    B.   His brains were so mushy he fancied himself some ski-slope stud, which would mean that

        1.   He was planning more ski trips with Ruth Carson.

        2.   He was planning more *without* her.

By the time I sat down, I was so disgusted with him, I had to remind myself that I hadn't seen him bring anything home except groceries and paint rollers and the like, which would mean that

    A.   He was buying clothes and keeping them in his office.

    B.   He was going to blow his money on over-priced stuff at some fancy resort shop.

By now I was downright indignant. Then it occurred to me that maybe

> C. He was going to go to a ski resort and
> look like a nerd in the clothes he already
> owned.

The man was my father. I couldn't endure the idea
of him being a laughingstock, even though he deserved it.

Then another thought assailed me. Was he planning to *rent* ski clothes when he got there? Did ski
shops at resorts rent more than skis and boots and
poles?

I couldn't ask him any of this. That would make
him think I was resigned to his going.

His name boomed over the loudspeaker, and he
went to pick up his order.

I grabbed Antony's hand and pulled my olives off
his fingers. "We do not wear other people's food.
And I don't even know when you last washed your
paws."

I glanced at Aida, who had looped my onion rings
over her ears.

"I'm a Princess," she said.

"You take those off or we're out of here!" Anarchy,
I thought. Mrs. Farisee is gone only days and we're

sinking into anarchy. And our own father is going away to let these two wallow in it.

When we got home, Herb, Joe, and Sadie came tumbling into the parlor to meet us. Poor Dow Jones just sat.

Bramwell had left a stainless steel dog bowl, a dog bed, dog vitamins, enough dog toys to stock a pet shop, and a dog seat-belt harness for riding in cars.

Dow Jones did not eat.

Dow Jones did not seem to mind that Sadie had appropriated his bed, and that Herb and Joe had fallen on his toys like wolves on a kill. He kept his distance, lying on the floor of the addition, his head between his paws, staring into some dark, private desolation.

When we'd first seen him, he'd been a skeleton of a dog. I could see that with Bramwell he'd been living the good life. His coat, which had been all but lost to starvation, had come back to about as good as it could be. Still, he was not what you'd call a handsome dog. His feet were uncommonly large for his size. Now that he was filled out . . . more than filled out, almost pudgy . . . he looked to be an amalgamation of mostly short and stocky breeds, but with the jowls and the mournful eyes of a blood-hound and the coarse, unruly coat of a terrier. While nobody could say he'd seen better years, he'd plainly seen a lot of years. His muzzle was already grizzled, the hair sticking up in all directions so that he looked as if he were peering through a gorse bush.

While any sensible person could see that this animal could stand to lose a few pounds, it worried me that he didn't eat.

It worried the twins at least as much.

"Oh, poor, poor dear. Oh, poor darling." Her arms around his chest, Aida buried her face in his neck.

This animal had dignity. He looked away, like a noble prisoner determined to withstand whatever horrors his jailers would inflict.

"Here you go, boy. Hey. Here you go." Antony shoved a dog biscuit under the dog's nose.

Dow Jones looked at my father as if to say, "Have you considered taking them to obedience training?"

"Okay," my father said. "Leave him alone."

"But he is sad. He is grieving," my sister protested.

"I could play him my harmonica," Antony offered.

"Either leave him alone or he goes to a kennel." I knew my father was bluffing, but the twins weren't so sure.

They went to their room. Since *Dracula's Daughter* was on a non-network channel, I figured they'd be watching it with the sound off until my father caught on.

I sat on the floor in the addition, just in case Dow Jones might appreciate the company of somebody who knew how he felt but didn't harass him.

He plodded to the door and stood stock-still. When I let him out into the fenced yard, he trudged to the gate and sat, looking at me imploringly.

"Trust me," I told him. "You'd never make it to Chicago. Keep thinking of the upside. There are many dogs who would be in heaven having kids and dogs to frolic with." Wrong note, I told myself. This dog is not a frolicker.

Dow Jones sat pining for Bramwell Grove. I doubt if even Bramwell's mother had ever missed him so desperately.

Sherman brought our vegetarian posters to school.

"They're great," I said. "They'll surely make people think about how food animals suffer, and how stupid it is to kill them and eat them for *Christmas*, of all times."

Sherman looked solemn and pleased. "Elliot did a lot on them, too."

He didn't bring the posters to lunch. Kerri and

Teena, Laurelle and Marti were already at their table when he and I joined them.

The minute we sat down, Kerri declared, as if announcing the results of a national ballot, "We've been thinking, Dez. You're supposed to give people a housewarming as soon as they move in. If we wait until after Christmas, there'll be New Year's, and then it'll be almost a month since you moved in."

Teena nodded. "So we thought, how about this weekend?"

"My dad will be . . . away . . . until Sunday afternoon." I couldn't understand why Laurelle hadn't told them, unless she was beginning to be embarrassed about the tryst aspect of her mother and him going.

"Perfect!" Marti said. "It can be a surprise housewarming! See, if we make it a surprise, and for him, too, he's not going to tell us we can't do it. *And* we can invite some adults, so he knows it's partly for him."

"If it's partly for him, we have to." Laurelle was firm.

Not only had she not vetoed the date, she was plainly in on the picking of it!

Kerri leaned toward me, as if to nail down the core of the strategy. "That way, Mike and those guys won't get there and see it's just a bunch of twelve-year-old girls, and book out."

Laurelle nodded, sage and sure. "My sister will be there anyway. If we have her *and* some adults, Mike and his friends will think more people her age will be coming, so they'll be sure to stay."

"Yeahhhh," Sherman breathed, awed. "That Sunday, *she'll* be there." The thought jolted him right out of his normal quiet around this group. "I can bring some great leftovers from the shindig my folks are having Saturday night." The offer was shy, but deeply felt.

There was silence. I could see that inviting Sherman hadn't occurred to any of the others.

"His parents' leftovers are classier than most people's holiday dinners." Even though I wasn't going to agree to Sunday, I wasn't going to let them plan anything in front of Sherman and not include him. While the date was all wrong, I was feeling more excited by the event every second. Here were my friends giving me a *party*. Never mind dissecting their motivations. I was going to be the guest of honor, along with my father. And with him working so hard moving and cleaning, shopping and painting, I couldn't help feeling a twinge of sympathy for the man.

Nobody had ever given him a party so far as I could remember. After my mother left us, and he lost his practice as a family counsellor, nobody gave him so much as a brunch. After he lost his job as a car salesman, nobody threw him even a coffee break.

I knew I should veto the day firmly, but I didn't want to kill everybody's enthusiasm.

Here it was, Christmas coming, with a new house, Mrs. Farisee gone, no friends to walk to school with. Just talking about *my* party took some of the chill off my life.

Marti, Kerri, Laurelle, and Teena were volunteering to bring drinks and nuts and pretzels and cups.

They were talking as if Sunday were definite. I'm not sure how it got away from me. I knew I should have stopped them and changed the date, but I guess I was afraid that if we put it off they might lose interest, that it might never happen.

Mob psychology, maybe. I never thought I was a person who could be easily influenced, but, then, I had never faced people giving me a housewarming before. The more they planned, the more it seemed to me that my father couldn't possibly object.

"Okay. Okay." Teena was all business. "So what adults are we going to invite?"

"Shirley Miller," Sherman said immediately.

Men. Even Sherman, good old Sherman, wasn't capable of being faithful to only one woman.

"Sherman." I tried to be patient. "She used to date my dad!"

Laurelle looked uneasy.

"But she dumped him for my uncle," Sherman assured everybody at the table.

I reminded myself that he was contributing gourmet leftovers. "So what makes you think she'd come without Bramwell?"

He shrugged. "Can you see anybody putting up with my uncle for months on end?"

I could feel my neck muscles tighten as I kept my voice civilized. "Sure. Sure. Invite everybody my father ever dated. Pat Troup. Or you want to really screw up the party, Irene Vardis."

There are times when anything you do, anything you say, backfires.

"Pat Troup?" Marti echoed. "Pat Troup the *reporter*?"

"Wow!" Kerri breathed. "A reporter at the party."

"She's not going to *write* about it," Teena said. "She covers heavy stuff like politics."

"Listen, she might. Even if she doesn't, a *reporter* at your housewarming . . ." Kerri was plainly beginning to see this party as even more than a way to meet Mike, as an event of glamour and high style, and her very own creation.

I glanced at Laurelle, trying to gauge how upset

she was. I couldn't tell from her face how she felt, and she didn't say anything.

She's not going to speak up and veto Sherman's goofy ideas, I realized. Okay. Let her mother meet my father's ex-dates. It will at least give Ruth Carson a better idea of his history, before she's in too deep.

Then it occurred to me that maybe Laurelle was too embarrassed to object to all these relics of my father's past.

I wasn't sure what I should do.

"And Langley Morris and Aunt." Sherman was no longer the shy nerd who never spoke up around this group. Sherman had the bit between his teeth, and Sherman was absolutely sure who should be invited. "Ms. Dettweiler. Mona and Lisa."

"Mona Lisa?" Teena echoed.

"Mona *and* Lisa," Laurelle told her. "You know, the Mona Lisa Salon de Beauté in the Rancho Grande Mall."

There are times when your best friends are among your greatest trials. The Rancho Grande Mall was one of Bramwell Grove's more run-down real estate holdings, and I didn't want anybody sneering at the place I got my hair cut.

"They were the first shop owners to let us put vegetarian posters in their window for Thanksgiving," Laurelle went on.

"If we ask them, shouldn't we invite the man where Mrs. Farisee took our shoes to be repaired?" I wondered.

Sherman didn't hesitate. "Nah. Repairing shoes isn't personal like cutting hair."

Before he could go on, Kerri got down to the heavy business of this party. "Who's going to invite Mike and his friends?"

"Might as well let Sherman," Marti said. "He knows everybody."

Sherman Grove. When I moved to this town only months earlier, he trailed me everywhere because kids his age teased him and called him a wimp. Now he was running "Lifestyles of the Rich and Famous."

"Great." Laurelle seemed to have no worries about all my father's old flames meeting her mother. "He sees Mike and those guys all the time."

"Okay." Marti looked at Sherman with even more respect. "So you do all the inviting. I mean, it'll be us, Mike and his friends, and those adults."

"Who else from our school?" I asked.

Everybody but Sherman looked at me as if I were so dense that the only kind thing was to ignore my question.

I was dumbfounded, but only for a minute. These girls had not gotten to be the most popular group in junior high without having some idea of *strategy*.

Now Sherman was the center of the planning. "You'll have to do it right away," Teena admonished him, then turned to the rest of us. "And be sure nobody lets a word leak out! A housewarming has to be a surprise party."

"No problem," Sherman assured her.

I could have pointed out that it would hardly be one to me, but this was no time to be snide.

Still, I felt as if I'd let things get away from me. How could this event have become a juggernaut in such a short time? If I tried to stop it now, or even postpone it, wouldn't I be deflating all this enthusiasm? Wouldn't I be shooting down all these great plans? Wouldn't I risk having everybody's attention shift to something else after Christmas?

When Faye Brower promised to do the posters for the school play and then backed out, nobody spoke to her for weeks. And now they only tolerated her for her sister's batons.

Nerd Sherman may be, but when he's sure about something he plows right ahead. I couldn't help wondering, though, how he would handle having two women he was dazzled by at the party. Maybe Sherman was too caught up in the juggernaut to worry about details. For the first time since I'd known him, he was accepted, included, in a group—and such a group.

"Make sure Mike doesn't tell Preston." I think that it was at this moment I gave up all my reservations. Run down by the juggernaut, now I was hanging on to it. "Otherwise, you can bet Preston will tell Antony, and Antony doesn't keep secrets worth anything." Even asserting myself this much made me feel a little more in control, so I went on. "And no presents. My father would have a fit if I helped plan my own surprise party and had the guests bring gifts."

"You're right," Teena said. "It would look really tacky."

Kerri nodded. "Besides, you can't have a last-minute party and expect people to rush out and buy you something."

"Especially not when it's almost Christmas," Marti agreed. "If you spring an invitation on them that means wading into all the crowds and hassle, they probably wouldn't come."

"Everybody's probably tapped out with buying Christmas presents anyway," Laurelle added.

"Okay, then," Sherman said. "No presents."

"*Absolutely* no presents," Teena told him. "You've got to be firm on that. Nothing from anybody."

I was relieved, but maybe a little disappointed, that everybody agreed with me so readily.

After school, Sherman showed up at my locker with Elliot.

Laurelle had come a long way from being one of the most popular girls in school. Elliot Lofting was somebody your average popular person would never let herself be seen with. And Laurelle walked out of school with the three of us without even trying to look as if we weren't really together. There was a lot to admire about Laurelle.

We hit all the places that had let us put up vegetarian Thanksgiving posters in their windows, then we stuck some of our Christmas posters on bulletin boards, ending up at the Rancho Grande Mall.

Mona and Lisa had let us put up our Thanksgiving posters mainly to irk Bramwell Grove, but now they were getting interested in the messages. I don't know how anybody who knows the suffering food animals go through can help caring, but most people manage.

Mona peered at the recipes. "Tofu, huh. Nutritional yeast . . ."

"The tofu you can get at any market," I assured her. "And any co-op or health food store will have the yeast. It makes great gravy."

"So, listen," Sherman said. "We're having a surprise housewarming for Dez Sunday at two, and we want you both to come."

Mona looked at me. "She's standing here."

"I know," he said. "She knows about it, but it's also a surprise for her dad."

"And you want us to come." Lisa looked as wary as Mona.

"As guests. As guests," I added hastily, remembering that Bramwell had put the arm on them to work at the party where I made the dog food canapes.

"What are you going to be serving?" Mona asked.

"Listen, if you're nervous about that, there'll be plenty of nuts and pretzels and stuff you can trust," Sherman said sincerely.

"Yeah. Well. Wow." Lisa looked pleased. They were pretty neat people, not to assume that if kids invited them it was going to be a dumb event.

"Be sure not to bring presents," Laurelle told them. "Absolutely no presents."

And there was Elliot Lofting standing there with us in his brown polyester slacks and brown loafers with Argyle socks, holding our vegetarian posters.

What could I do? "So, Elliot, of course you're coming."

"I already asked him," Sherman said.

I'll give it to Laurelle. When we put up the last

poster and Elliot started home, she said, "See you, Elliot."

She may be a royal pain about her mother's love life, I thought, but she's got a good heart.

My father spent the evening painting the kitchen and parlor.

After Antony sneezed into the paint while it was being stirred, my father, his face flecked with Premium Flat Coat, told me to keep the twins anyplace but in the vicinity of him or his work.

"You'd better wash your glasses," I advised. While I hadn't forgiven him, I didn't want his vision so screwed up he'd make a mess of our walls.

The twins and I threw a ball around the backyard for the dogs. Herb and Joe and Sadie kept skidding into Dow Jones, trying to involve him, but only making him more depressed.

At least the walls of the main rooms would look good for the party, I thought. If only a party could cheer up a downcast dog.

6

We were a few blocks from the grade school Friday morning when Antony spied Preston and his crowd straggling along behind Sherman and Mike and Mike's friends.

"Can you let us out here?" Antony begged my father.

It was fine with me. I missed walking to school with old Sherman, and I knew my brother must miss Preston. Aida was the one I worried about, changed from afternoon to morning session. With any luck, I thought, one or two of Preston's friends will take a liking to her.

As we climbed out of the car, Preston and Sherman caught up with us.

"Remember," my father told me, "I'm going to pick up Antony and Aida early and take them to Ruth's. You and Laurelle can walk there, and then Nicole will drive you all up to our house."

"Can I come?" Sherman asked me as my father drove away.

"*May* I come." I knew I sounded like a parent, but I didn't want to hurt his feelings with a fast, flat no, or by telling him I could not bear to ride in any car with him *yearning* over Nicole.

As Antony walked on with Preston and his gang, Aida lagging a little behind, Mike and his friends joined us.

"There's probably no room in the car," I told Sherman. "And you wouldn't have any way to get home."

Sherman does not let logistics stand in the way of a fixed idea. "Mike, would you like to drive up and see Dez's new house after school?"

Mike's friends walked on, deep in a discussion about video laser disks.

"Sherman," I said, as calmly as I could, "Nicole Carson is sixteen years old. She probably doesn't even consider you a life-form."

"Nicole Carson?" Mike's voice was awed. "Nicole Carson is going to be at your house?"

"You know what males are? Males are an entirely different species." I walked on, alone.

"It is absolutely sickening," I told Laurelle as we went down to lunch at noon. "Sherman asked Mike to drive him up to our house after school just because your *sister* is going to be there, and you'd think he asked Mike to come visit Madonna or something."

Laurelle stopped dead. "Mike *Harbinger*? Mike Harbinger is coming to your house today? Oh, my gosh. Don't tell anybody. Don't *mention* it until after, or everybody will find a way to get up there. Oh, guy! And I'm getting a zit on my chin!"

Teena, Marti, and Kerri were already at the usual table. Laurelle grabbed my arm. "Don't say anything!"

I sat down, thinking that the whole human race was a screwed up proposition. And, party or no party, I was still an outsider. Here was practically everybody I knew, even my own father, tangled up in romantic situations, or fantasies, and I was not involved in any of it. Good, I thought. Good. I hope I never fall in love. It makes people too ridiculous.

The minute Sherman sat down, everybody wanted to know who was coming Sunday.

"Mike will be there," I declared, before Sherman

could answer. "And if they heard Sherman mention Nicole, you can bet all his friends will be, too."

Laurelle was waiting outside my last class. "Let's hurry, so nobody tags along."

Walking to her house, she asked, "When is he picking up Sherman?"

"He has to go home for his folks' car, Laurelle. He doesn't come equipped with a winged chariot."

"Oh, good. I'll have time to change."

The minute we hit her house, she rushed to her room and started ransacking her closet, throwing clothes on her bed. "Does this make me look older? How about this? No. It makes me look chunky."

"Just pack whatever you'll need."

"I packed yesterday. But I didn't know Mike would be coming up *today!*" She shoved her face almost against the mirror over her dresser. "Guy! With these eyelashes I look like Sissy Spacek in *Carrie*. Listen, do you think I'd look phony with mascara?"

"Laurelle, you have to have practice to put on mascara."

"I was on the makeup committee for the school play."

"And you were a nervous wreck for fear you'd put somebody's eye out."

She sucked in her cheeks. "Blusher. What I need is blusher."

"*Laurelle!*" I think I kept cool longer than most people my age would have. "Mike Harbinger is coming to my house because of your sister. Could we get something to drink?"

"Go help yourself."

Looking in the Carsons' immaculate refrigerator, I remembered that there'd been a time when I was as goofy as Laurelle and the rest of them over Mike. But I didn't even feel jealous. It occurred to me that I would have been scared to death if he'd ever felt romantic toward me. Having him as a friend wasn't scary. And maybe he was more than a friend. Maybe he'd been what I needed, with my mother gone and my father besotted with one woman after another and our housekeeper leaving. As for the twins, they were their own society, just the two of them. And Sherman was somebody I always felt needed looking after. Maybe Mike had become, besides my buddy, the big brother I needed.

Only now, he'd gotten as sotted as Sherman and my father.

When it came right down to it, the only people I had to rely on were our dogs.

I trudged back down the hall with two cans of soda as Laurelle was coming out of the bathroom.

I stopped. "Oh, wow. How did you bruise your cheeks?"

"That's contouring, Dez."

"You want an opinion?"

"No." Then she softened. "So what about my eye-liner?"

"It looks as if your eyes are wearing moustaches." She stalked into the bathroom.

I sat on her bed with the sodas. I hated to hurt her feelings. But was I supposed to lie to my best friend? Was I supposed to let her look like *The Rocky Horror Picture Show*?

She trailed into the room, her face scrubbed.

"Believe me," I consoled her. "It's for the best. You don't want to madden Mike Harbinger beyond what you're prepared to cope with."

"That's not funny."

"Come on, Laurelle. You're twelve. He's sixteen. And Nicole would always be between you."

She slumped on the bed like a puppet whose strings had been clipped, but she was still careful not to sit on her clothes. "It's always that way. It's always been that way. From the time I can remember, everybody has gushed about how beautiful she is, while I stand there gathering flies. I guess I'll never get over thinking that just once somebody will see *me*. Then, of course, I think 'What's to see?' It's such a waste, you know. She's so used to being admired that she takes it for granted. She gets guys she doesn't even *want.*"

I pressed the soda into Laurelle's hand. "Do you suppose that's why she gets them? I mean, besides being incredibly gorgeous. Do you think maybe it's her attitude that works like a stun gun on males?"

"It can't be her personality. Living with her my whole life, I'd notice if she had one. Do you think it's because she acts as if she's *entitled* to everybody's adoration that she gets it?"

"How does your mom treat her?"

"About like she treats me. I don't think she sees what a total pill Nicole is. But she doesn't let her get away with her royalty act."

No matter how dumb Laurelle was being, I had to feel sorry for her, imagining what it would be like to have Nicole for a sister. I was careful to look neutral when Laurelle layered on some of her sister's lip gloss. There's a limit to the helpful criticism you can lay on anybody.

"I know my mom hasn't a clue about the party," she assured me, dabbing Nicole's perfume on her wrist. "So if your dad drops her off and then comes to your house, we'll have to phone her to come up."

We went into the bathroom where Laurelle

searched the medicine cabinet for tooth whitener.

Nicole arrived a little while later. Ignoring me, she looked at her sister's lips. "Been eating lard?" She sauntered to her room.

"Do you think more sculpting glaze would make my hair look too stiff?" Laurelle asked me.

It did.

We had to rinse her head and start all over with a mousse and her mother's hair dryer.

Laurelle looked in the mirror. "Maybe I can borrow Nicole's crimping iron."

"Your head is about to turn into a Brillo pad," I assured her solemnly.

Ruth Carson came home with tapes of a couple of Disney movies and bags of fruit and graham crackers and bran muffins for us. I hadn't had so much wholesomeness dumped on me in years.

"My mother is kind of out of it," Laurelle confided, looking through the stuff.

Meanwhile, Mrs. Carson was hauling suitcases to her front stoop.

This woman, I thought, could take a few lessons in cool from her older daughter.

By the time my father arrived with the twins, Mrs. Carson had repeated all her instructions and cautions to us three times.

Antony and Aida stood with me, silently watching

my father and Ruth Carson load her luggage into our station wagon.

Ruth gave her keys to Nicole, who'd come out of the house looking like a French aristocrat about to ride to the guillotine, and went over everything she'd told Laurelle and me. Then my father had to repeat the same stuff.

Finally they drove away, leaving two sets of offspring standing there on the sidewalk, all but Laurelle looking as happy as a chain gang on a rainy day.

Nicole actually addressed me. "I suppose you're a vegetarian, too."

I nodded.

She peered at the twins. "Them?"

I was firm. "For this weekend they are."

"Friday night," Nicole muttered, as if cataloging the injustices heaped upon her. "Friday night, stuck with four rug rats, and all of them vegetarians."

She drove us to a Chinese restaurant, ordered us to stay in the car, and went in.

"It's against the law to leave kids alone in a car." Antony volunteered his first syllables since he'd arrived at the Carsons'.

"You're with us," Laurelle assured him. "Dez, you should have called Sherman to say we wouldn't be there until . . ."

"You're kids, too," Antony told her.

"You mean if the police come, they'll arrest our father?" Aida was uneasy.

"He's away," Antony intoned darkly. "Besides, it's not his car. It belongs to that girl who's supposed to be watching us."

"*I'm watching you!*" I snarled through my teeth.

"If the restaurant gets held up and the robbers hi Mack this car to get away in, and they arrest that girl along with the robbers, who's going to drive us home?" Aida asked.

"We should be ready to jump out of the car if we see any masked guys running out of the restaurant," Antony advised her.

"Listen, Dez, you don't have to tell Mike how old I am," Laurelle said.

"No, if we jump out of the car the police might think we're part of the gang and arrest us all," Aida told her brother.

"Should I act as if I know who he is, or do you kind of introduce us, or what?" Laurelle pressed.

Antony's hand fell like a pebble on my shoulder. "If we get arrested, *who's going to feed the dogs?*"

There I was, having something in common with Nicole again. We seemed to be the only two who even *noticed* we'd been abandoned.

As Nicole pulled into our driveway, I realized just

how isolated our new house was. There were no neighbors' houses in sight. Even though it was barely six, the light was gone to gray.

Then I saw that our place was not deserted. There was another car in our driveway.

Mike had managed to borrow his father's red Lexus instead of their family station wagon.

As we got out of the Carsons' Ford, Nicole strode back to the trunk. "You're not allowed to have company," she told me.

Sherman was at her side in a moment. "I'm not company. I'm always at the Blanks'. Could I take your luggage or anything?"

She lifted out her bag.

Laurelle stood there with her suitcase and the bag of supplies from her mother. I stood holding a leaking sack of Chinese food.

"This is Sherman Grove, whose family happens to own this house, Nicole." I shoved the sack into his hand and took Laurelle's suitcase.

Ignoring the fact that he had sweet-and-sour sauce running down his wrist, Nicole handed her lavender cassette player to Sherman, not even glancing at Mike, who stood thunderstruck.

She walked back to the driver's door of the car. "I'm going down to the mall and rent some movies," she told Laurelle.

Laurelle managed to take her eyes off Mike. "You're only supposed to leave here in an emergency."

"Believe me, being stuck up in this place all weekend is an emergency." And then a remote but chilling suspicion struck Nicole. She fixed me with a narrow gaze. "You *do* have a VCR?"

There was no way around it. I would have to confess to this person that we lacked such a basic.

"I do," Mike said quickly. "I can go get it."

"This is Mike Harbinger," I told Nicole. While I was as disgusted with him as with Sherman, I wanted her to know this tall, gorgeous blond high school hotshot was *my* friend.

"Haven't I seen you around school?" Mike asked.

"I wouldn't know." All four of Nicole's brain cells were focused on a truly profound concern, the VCR problem.

"Haven't I seen you around school?" Right up there with "Do you come here often?" or "What's your sign?" I thought.

"My folks have a whole library of movies," Sherman offered. "I can bring up just about anything you like. Or I could rent anything we don't have."

I will find a nunnery, I decided. I will sign up in advance. Here is my own father acting like some kind of rounder . . . or is it bounder? Here is Sherman, a genius, a kid with more conscience than anybody I know, and Mike, the most popular guy in high school, *devastated* by this twit of a Nicole, who is maybe as deep as her nail gloss.

On the other hand, here is Laurelle, standing with braised tofu and vegetable chow mein leaking from Sherman's bag onto her shoes, gawking at Mike, who wouldn't notice her if she were twirling batons between her teeth with her hair on fire.

"You know you can't be driving around wherever you take a notion in Mom's car." From being struck dumb by Mike's presence, Laurelle found her voice in a desperate effort to spend an evening watching movies with Mike, even if Sherman and Nicole and the twins and I were there.

A person can be so shallow she's mysterious. I don't know what made Nicole back down, but she handed her bag to Mike and snapped her fingers at me. "Door key."

I unlocked my front door. I took Nicole's bag from Mike, and thrust it at her. "Let me show you where you'll sleep," I told her, and walked down the hall to my father's room.

He'd got a new double bed with a regular bedspread, new draperies, and a decent secondhand dresser before he left. Tossing her bag on the bed, Nicole looked around the room. "This is it?"

"Yeah. If we'd known sooner that you were coming, we would have called in a decorator."

As I headed back to the parlor, I heard Aida open the door to the addition.

Yelping as if they'd been confined for months, Herb, Joe, and Sadie scrambled in, knocked down the twins, and licked their faces frantically.

Then they charged me, leaping and twisting as if snatching for invisible Frisbees. They rolled on their backs, tongues lolling out, then sprang up to greet Sherman, planting their paws on his shoulders and lapping his face.

Dow Jones stayed out in the service yard.

The noise must have tweaked Nicole's curiosity. She emerged from my father's room. "Whose are *those*?" she demanded, recoiling from the animals.

"Mine," I said firmly.

The dogs stood still, looking at her.

Once I saw a film on cable TV at Sherman's, *In Praise of Wolves*. In it, a man who lived around wolves said he was certain they had ESP.

I suspect all canines do.

As if Nicole weren't present, Herb, Joe, and Sadie strolled over to inspect Mike. He sat down on the floor, and in a minute they were all wrestling around together.

Poor Dow Jones lay outside, not even getting within ESP range.

"Heat up the dinners and put those animals out," Nicole told Laurelle over the pandemonium. "And then your friends will have to leave."

The girl had manners to match her charm.

She went back into my father's room.

Even the twins sensed the chill left in her wake. "Want to look at our swimming pool?" Antony asked Mike.

I was grateful for anything to break the silence. But I warned, "You don't want to right now. It . . . uh . . . it won't be seeable until summer."

"But cleaned up it will be great!" Laurelle was going to do anything she could to keep Mike Harbinger there.

"You have to see it!" Sherman agreed. "It's all slimy and decayed like a horror movie."

Assertiveness, I thought. I have to master assertiveness, or I'm going to be run down by well-meaning juggernauts all my life. Now is the time to say firmly, "We will not go up to the pool tonight." But I didn't have the heart, after the way Nicole had behaved.

Sherman shut the dogs in the garage. "I don't want to have to fish them out of that slimy mess if they fall in."

At least Mike wouldn't be disappointed by the pool, I thought.

Even though the day had been warm for December, the evening was clear and cold, with a white moon already rising. My father had put a floodlight in the fixture over the back door, so that we were able to see where we walked.

From the garage, the dogs' howls rose in a mournful, eerie chorus.

It felt precarious, picking our way up steps dappled by the dark shadows of the trees and the bushes. I held the twins' hands tight, thinking that this was the perfect setting for a mad slasher movie.

"It looks repulsive now, but as soon as spring comes I'm going to get in there and clean it out. . . ." What am I doing? I thought. Am I apologizing because I'm afraid once Mike sees it he'll never want to come back and swim? Apologizing to the friend with whom I have fed dog food snacks to the most powerful people in town?

"You," I told the twins, "remember, you're never to go *near* the pool enclosure without Dad or me."

The solar fixture lit the pool deck, leaving the bushes around it in darkness.

Sherman reached for the gate latch. "Dez, you have to be careful about leaving the gate unlocked like this. If anybody ever got in and broke a neck in the pool, you'd never forgive yourself."

"I didn't unlock it." I stepped through the gate, and then stopped, holding the twins' wrists tighter.

"Hey!" Mike murmured.

"Fan*tas*tic!" Laurelle gasped.

The deck was swept and scrubbed, the pool without a leaf or a speck of mold on its clear blue surface.

"Sherman!" Even in my imagination, I'd not pictured anything this beautiful, this glamorous. "Sherman, your uncle must have ordered it cleaned."

"The only way my uncle would pay to have that pool scrubbed is if he planned to fill it with crocodiles and show it to people who owed him money."

"But who?" I turned to Laurelle.

"Us? My mom went into hock for ski clothes."

"Nobody in her right mind would have a pool cleaned in December anyway," Sherman declared.

Glorious as the pool and the terrace looked, I couldn't ignore the mystery of how it happened. "Okay. I know we didn't have it cleaned. Nobody I can think of offhand had it done. Mrs. Farisee would never have—she disapproved of the whole place. Then *who did it?*"

"Do you suppose neighbors ordered pool service

and gave the wrong address?" Laurelle wondered.

Mike shook his head. "Sherman's right. Nobody's going to have an outdoor, uncovered pool cleaned in midwinter."

"Maybe somebody did it as a practical joke," Laurelle offered. "There are warped people, you know."

"Do you know what it must have cost to dredge out that mess and scrub it?" Sherman countered. "Nobody's going to spend that kind of money on a practical joke that *improves* something."

"They did in that Shirley Temple movie where her father went to war and left her in the mean boarding school," Aida reminded him. "And the man in the turban climbed in the window and—"

" 'Sarah . . . Sarah . . .' " Antony quavered, closing his eyes and feeling around him with his free hand.

"Cut it out," I muttered automatically. By now I was feeling downright uneasy. "But it's almost spooky not knowing who did it."

"Dez!" Laurelle was not one for heavy speculation. "We could have the party up here! The weather's great, and there's so much more room than in the parlor, and we wouldn't have to worry about anybody spilling anything!"

Sherman nodded, all enthused. "This would be a

lot classier! Your parlor furniture is pretty crummy, Dez."

"What a place for a party!" Mike said. "Besides, whoever had the pool cleaned might pass by and see all the action and drop in, and then you'd know who it was."

"Of course, we'll have to fill it," Laurelle pointed out. "It wouldn't look right to have a pool party around an empty pool."

"We could do it tomorrow," Mike said.

"Better wait until first thing Sunday morning," Sherman said. "That way you won't have a lot of dead leaves and stuff on the water."

It was an odd feeling standing on that deck in the light of the solar fixture in mid-December, talking about my pool party. Here was a daydream taking form months ahead of schedule! There'd be time enough later to worry about who had hurried things up by having the pool and deck cleaned.

"We're having a party?" Aida cried.

"Can I invite Preston?" Antony asked.

"And Tran!" Aida added. "Tran has to come."

I was jolted back to the moment, and ashamed of myself. I had just assumed that the twins would be *around* for the housewarming; it hadn't occurred to me that they'd be involved, or that they deserved to have their own guests. "Tran's mother would never let her come alone. And they don't have a car." Then I thought, no, some way I have to get their friends here.

Aida looked up at Mike. "If you come, could you bring them?"

"I guess so." Mike was a pushover for a heartfelt appeal. It almost made up for him being a pushover for a perfect face.

"I need to go call Tran," Aida said.

"We forgot the dinners in the oven!" Laurelle gasped.

As we hurried down to the kitchen, Mike assured Antony that yes, he would certainly remember to bring Preston, too.

I'd set the alarm for seven the next morning. Laurelle and the twins were so excited that they got to work right after breakfast, putting things away in drawers and cupboards and unearthing more things for the housewarming. While Laurelle vacuumed, the twins dusted and I stashed the junk they'd dug out and salvaged the things we needed from the drawers and cupboards they'd stuffed them into.

The vacuuming must have wakened Nicole.

She came wandering into the kitchen at eleven. "Can't a person get any *sleep* around here?"

"If they do it before noon," I told her.

She opened the refrigerator. "*Soy* milk? This is

like being stuck in some Yoga commune."

She heated a frozen waffle and trailed back to my father's room with it.

Sherman and Mike arrived a little after noon, with Preston. "We thought you might need some help setting up for the party," Sherman explained.

Laurelle fled to my room, while Antony and Aida immediately took Preston to theirs.

"My folks went to a wedding out of town, so I'm stuck with Preston all day and tonight," Mike said.

He was mopping the kitchen floor when Laurelle came out wearing a new sweater and a skirt, her hair as smooth and stiff as an Annette Funicello doll's. A skirt yet. The only other time I'd seen her in a skirt was the night of the school play.

"I thought maybe we could hang out up here after we work, if it's okay with you," Mike said from the kitchen. "I brought my VCR and some tapes. I can baby-sit Preston for a few hours, but then he gets . . ."

Nicole emerged from my father's room.

Sherman and Mike stood speechless, Sherman with the window squeegee, Mike clutching the mop.

Passing them as if they were hired help in whom one didn't want to encourage familiarity, Nicole yanked open the refrigerator door. "There is absolutely nothing fit to eat in this place."

"My dad got a whole load of groceries," I told her firmly. "So did your mother."

"*Vegetarian*," she countered. "Or fruit and graham crackers. Or stuff that has to be *cooked*."

"We could all go get something downtown," Mike suggested.

Laurelle hurried to my room. She had her coat on before I even got there.

"How do I *look?*" she whispered while we buttoned the twins into their sweaters.

She looked flushed, but I knew that if I said so, she'd only get more nervous. "Fine."

When we were all outside, I locked the front door.

Nicole walked over to her mother's car. "Be back here by three," she ordered Laurelle.

"You're not coming with us?" Sherman sounded like the villager devastated that Conan or Zorro, after saving the population, isn't going to hang around.

"I have things to do." She got in the car and pulled away, leaving Mike stuck with his little brother, two twelve-year-old girls, an eleven-year-old nerd, and five-year-old twins.

Looking at Mike Harbinger, nobody would expect that, on top of all his gifts, he was unbelievably good-natured. "Listen, I wanted to ask you, if we're going to watch movies up here later, do you mind if we go get Wendell? I don't like to leave him alone too long."

"Yeah," Preston concurred. "He can't hold it long, so if we don't get him, we'll have to blot up where he widdles in the house."

Laurelle looked at me.

"Wendell is their dog," I explained. "And we will bring him, by all means. All this house needs is another dog."

Mike was too relieved to pick up on irony. "In that case, we should take yours to my house. If they meet him on his territory first, they're not going to hassle him on theirs."

"I would leash them all," Sherman advised, "just in case something goes wrong."

Antony looked worried but stern. "We'd better . . ."

"No," I said firmly. "Turnip kits will not be needed."

A big, gas-guzzling station wagon is socially irresponsible, I know, but in this case, with seven humans and four, then five, dogs to transport, it was useful. I wondered what Mike's parents would have thought about him hauling such a menagerie around. Luckily, the wagon's upholstery was already layered with Wendell's hair, so this was their dog-hauling vehicle.

What with being sat on and licked by the dogs, Laurelle wouldn't have had a chance to speak even if she'd been able to dredge up anything to say. Dow Jones sat on my lap, leaning against the door, looking as if he wished it would fly open and dump him on the road. I hoped Bramwell would never find out I didn't put his dog in the seat belt harness.

Sherman, of course, knew of a great coffeehouse that had all vegetarian food.

When I had such a terrible crush on Mike, I would never have imagined him hanging out with Sherman and Laurelle and me and three five-year-olds, blotting up spilled soy shakes and wiping miso off his brother's elbow.

I'd never had the nerve then to walk by the Harbingers' house. Now that Mike was just my friend, I didn't feel any need to. His neighborhood was as elegant as the Groves', but newer. Mike pulled up a long driveway to an enormous, sprawling ranch house, with a three-car garage and flagstone siding. He went in and brought out Wendell on a leash.

Wendell was all basset hound; I suspect he was born middle-aged, unhurried and philosophical.

Sensible dogs always behave appropriately. Had Wendell been a puppy, mine would have been all over him in a riot of romping. Sizing up Wendell as old and podgy, they sniffed him and let him sniff them, tried a few paw nudges, and then settled down.

There weren't even any stiff legs or hackles.

We put them all in the backyard, except for Dow Jones, who begged with his eyes to be left in the wagon.

Mike and Preston were delighted to see that Wendell had only wet a few places in the hall.

"He can't help it," Preston explained, wiping the carpet with old rags. "We don't yell at him. My father says that if he ever gets so old he pees all over the house, he wouldn't want anybody yelling at him."

"Blot," Mike ordered.

After Mike threw the damp rags in the washer, we browsed through the video tapes in the family room. Poor Laurelle was so overwhelmed by being with Mike Harbinger in Mike Harbinger's house that I doubt if she saw a single title.

"You gots any mummy movies?" Aida asked.

Preston looked at her, puzzled. I must say I was happy to see Preston puzzled; Preston was the most self-assured kid I had ever met. "Mummy movies?"

"Movies about mummies," Antony explained.

"What's a mummy?" Preston asked.

"*Well*," Antony said, "when a fairy died in ancient Egypt, first they took out all its insides . . ."

"No mummy movies," Mike said firmly.

"All its insides?" Preston urged Antony, as we went out to fetch the dogs and herd them into the wagon.

Getting the dogs into the station wagon was only a little more demanding than trying to control a buffalo stampede.

Clambering over the dogs, Antony went on explaining to Preston about mummies.

Aida climbed over Sadie to kiss poor Dow Jones, who tried to wedge himself behind me.

"Better open a window," Preston advised. "If we drive on a curvy road, Wendell's apt to throw up. So do you suppose you have to go to a school to learn how to do mummies?"

"Oh, no," Antony told him. "Sherman's done a million of them."

There was an old Land Rover in our driveway, the kind of vehicle you see bouncing across the African veldt in movies.

Maybe neighbors come to welcome us, I told myself. That's friendly of them. But I'm not supposed to say my father's not home, and I'm certainly not going to say he'll be back Sunday with some *woman*.

As I climbed out of the car, I heard voices up by the pool.

That Nicole, I thought. After she insults my friends she brings *hers* over.

But where was her mother's sedan?

"Leave the dogs in the car," I said. Maybe Nicole had had an accident and somebody drove her here. I should go up first to prepare Laurelle in case Nicole had been hurt, or was all shaken up. And we certainly couldn't loose a dog pack, however friendly, on anybody. I'd just walk up to the terrace and find out what was going on.

"Were you expecting somebody?" Mike asked me.

What if it didn't turn out to be Nicole, or neighbors?

"Let's check it out," I said. Though I knew there had to be some non-sinister reason for voices at the pool area, it was good to have friends with me.

As we got closer to the terrace, I could make out what sounded like half a dozen voices, all of them speaking a strange tongue.

The pool gate was ajar. The pool was full of water. On the terrace were scattered towels and blankets, thermos jugs, and three enormous iron basins full of charcoal, glowing in places, tiny flames leaping from the gray and ruddy chunks.

There were also eight Asian men in swimming briefs stretching and doing breathing exercises.

While eight strange unclothed men standing

around your swimming pool in December is unnerving, those iron braziers full of burning coals made me edge closer to my friends. Scraps of thought, images scuttled through my mind . . . blood sacrifices, unspeakable rituals, unclean spirits . . .

"What are they doing without their clothes?" my sister demanded, scandalized.

There was no sign of Nicole.

For all my shock, I could not run away, or scream, or call 911. Like most people, I'm scared to death of looking ridiculous. If these men were not up to some evil, I'd be making a terrible fool of myself.

Nevertheless, this was my house, and my pool. "Are you . . . somebody's company?" I asked.

Mike stepped through the gate. "Do any of you speak English?"

"Of course," the shortest man replied.

The rest of us followed Mike onto the deck.

"Where's my sister?" So it had occurred to Laurelle, too, that something might have happened to Nicole.

The men looked at one another in bewilderment.

"Who's with you? Who invited you?" Mike asked, calm but firm.

"Nobody else is with us. Nobody invited us," a tall man said.

"Wait a minute." Sherman stepped around me. "You guys are from the pool service, right?"

Of course, I thought, relieved. But that brought up another problem. Who was paying for all this work? I imagined us getting the bill. "We didn't order the pool cleaned, or filled," I told the men.

"Order?" the tall man looked confused. "No one ordered us. We have to scrub and fill it in order to swim in it."

"Oh, wait." I was stunned by their nerve, but I knew it was my job to set them straight. "You can't come up here and take over a stranger's pool!"

"No, no." The short man, who seemed to be the group's leader, spoke up again. "This is our pool. We have leashed it."

"Leashed it," the tall man murmured.

"Oh, boy," Sherman muttered.

"*Leased?*" Mike was stern. "Who leased it to you?"

The eight men conferred. Then one went back down the path toward the parking pad.

I had no idea how a person should deal with eight strange men who were standing around her swimming pool claiming they'd leased it.

Aida pulled on my sleeve. "Can we swim, too?"

"What about my sister?" Laurelle edged closer to me.

"Your sister?" The tall man was attentive, obviously trying to be polite despite his bewilderment.

"You didn't just come up here on your own. You didn't just pass the place at random and decide it would be a good place to swim." Mike was stern. "You can't even see it from the street."

"Oh, no. We have been looking some time for a pool," the leader said.

"*Why?*" Sherman asked.

"We have been studying in the United States and training for the Chinese swimming team for years, planning some day to represent China in a summer Olympics. Then . . ." He was silent.

The tallest man spoke, very quietly. "Then, after the massacre at Tiananmen Square, we could not return to China. We had been very active in the freedom movement here. So we continue our studies here, we do what freedom work we can, and we continue training for the Olympics, waiting for the day we can return home. When our money ran low, we transferred to the college here, where the tuition and living costs are far less. But this college has no swimming pool open in winter."

The leader went on. "We were at a café, discussing the problem, when a man sitting down the counter moved closer. He offered to find a swimming pool for us. He did, and he leased it to us for a hundred dollars a month."

"Wait a minute. Wait a minute." Sherman looked grim. "You paid this guy in advance?"

The man nodded.

"Tall, handsome, black hair, drives a dark blue Maserati?"

"Oh, no," the leader said. "He is not even my height, plump, with yellow hair. He rode a bicycle."

Sherman looked relieved.

"So are we going to swim now?" Antony asked.

"You don't want to swim in the cold," Preston told him. "You could get carbuncles."

Antony took Preston almost as seriously as Preston took himself. "Car bumpers?"

"Buncles, *buncles*," Preston told him urgently. "All coughing and guck in your lungs."

"He means bronchitis," Mike said absently as the man who'd gone down the path handed him a paper.

"So, bronchitis," Preston told Antony. "If you get it and die before Christmas everybody would have to take your presents back for a refund."

"Or stuff you with them, if they take out your insides," Aida observed.

They went on to debate whether Antony should be wound in gift wrap.

The document Mike held said that in exchange for $100 a month rent, the Chinese Men's Students' Olympic Swim Team had leased the swimming pool at 1373 Hillcrest. The paper was signed *John Doe* and *Fong Li.*

"Wow. A genuine hand-printed contract," Laurelle observed wryly.

"Oh, man," Mike told the swim team. "You were had."

"Had?" the leader asked. "I signed it myself."

"John Doe is a phony name for nobody in particular," I explained.

"I suspect whoever conned you has been prowling around this place and noticed that it was vacant and had a pool," Mike told the team.

I was relieved, but only a little. "Then whoever it was hasn't been around to notice that anybody's moved in. So at least it's not a neighbor."

"Maybe just a neighbor's friend or relative," Laurelle observed.

Much as I liked her, she could be uncommonly irritating.

Sherman drew Mike and me aside. Naturally, Laurelle and Preston and the twins followed.

"They did a great job on the pool," Sherman said. "And they're out a hundred dollars to boot."

I looked past him at the glowing charcoal in the bowls. "What . . ."

"For heat," Sherman told me. "They even lugged this stuff up here."

Mike put an arm around my shoulder. "Myself, I'd let them use the pool. I mean, we couldn't do anything about the Chinese government massacre of all those students in Tiananmen Square, but this is a very small way of . . ."

"Of sticking with them," Sherman said.

Even Laurelle, who was struck dumb by the sight of Mike's arm on my shoulder, managed to nod.

It made sense to me. Still, I was worried about anybody swimming in this weather. We were warm enough in sweaters, but the water had to be cold. The charcoal warmed the air for only a few feet around each basin.

I walked back to the team. "You'll freeze in the water."

"Oh, no," Fong Li said. "Let me show you."

Before I could stop him, he dived into the pool. I turned to his friends. "Somebody get him out of there!"

The tall man smiled at me reassuringly. "No problem."

Not a man on the team showed the slightest concern.

Fong Li was a great swimmer, graceful and powerful.

"I'm going to feel terrible if he gets cramps and sinks," Laurelle told me.

"If he drowns," Aida asked, "will they take out . . ."

"No." I didn't want to know what she might ask. I was about to order Fong Li out of the water, when he boosted himself over the coving and stood, smiling, not even shivering, no tinge of blue on his lips.

"*Man!*" Sherman whispered.

Fong Li picked up a towel. "You see, you concentrate on a spot about an inch behind your nasal."

"Navel," the tall man said.

"Yes." Fong Li pointed to his belly button. "When you can keep your concentration there, you can control your response to heat and cold."

Sherman was enthralled. "That's Yoga, right?"

The tall man shook his head. "No. Yoga is a discipline from India."

"Can I try it?" Antony asked me.

"Never." I held his wrist tight, just to be sure.

Sherman was solemn. "Not many people have a Chinese Men's Students' Yoga Olympic Swim Team in their pool in December around here."

"Not Yoga. Yoga originated in India," another man corrected him.

"But it sounds so classy." Now that Mike's arm was off my shoulder, Laurelle was able to speak.

We sat around the charcoal, Antony on my lap, Aida on Laurelle's, Preston cuddled between Sherman and Mike, watching the team swim laps.

"Could you show me that controlling heat and cold thing?" Mike asked when they finally emerged from the pool.

"Of course," one of the men volunteered, without a shiver.

"But you don't master Yoga in a day," Sherman warned Mike.

I guess the team had given up on correcting him. Or, more likely, they were too polite to take issue with an eleven-year-old nerd.

After the swimmers left, we went back to Mike's car. Herb, Joe, and Sadie tumbled out, barking and wrestling one another. Of course, while we were up there confronting eight strangers, they hadn't made a sound. Mike boosted Wendell out of the car, then I lifted Dow Jones out.

Once in the house, Wendell lay down in the middle of the living room, as if exhausted by guarding the car. My dogs were so rowdy, racing around and roughhousing, I had to put them out.

Dow Jones followed. I guess, by now, he felt safer with them than with a strange dog.

We heard another car pull into the driveway. Laurelle looked out the window. "It's just my sister."

Nicole swept into the parlor. "Do you allow dogs in the parlor?" she asked me.

"Don't scratch and nobody will notice," I told her.

She strode past me and back to my father's room.

"We've got to go anyway." Mike gathered up Wendell and yelled for Preston.

"So we'll come a while before the party tomorrow," Sherman told Laurelle and me. "Mike's going to bring some stuff, too, since it's a housewarming."

Laurelle and I were cutting tofu into cubes when Nicole looked into the kitchen. "Are they gone?"

"Gone," Laurelle assured her.

"What are you doing?"

"We are making a fabulous dinner," Laurelle told her.

While vegetarians aren't pushy, it's a joy to lay a great vegetarian recipe on somebody. And everybody who gives up meat means more animals saved from misery and slaughter. "You cube the tofu," I explained. "Firm tofu. It has to be firm. Then you dredge the cubes in nutritional yeast."

"In *what*?"

Laurelle showed her the bowl of golden flakes. "You get it at the co-op, or a health food store. Tons of protein and vitamins, no fat."

The no fat part interested Nicole for a minute.

"Then you deep-fry it in canola oil," Laurelle added.

"You're talking no fat and then you deep-fry?" Nicole accused her.

"You don't have to fry it. You could broil it, or grill it." I had a position to defend. "Anyway, my father made me promise not to fry anything while he's away. We're going to . . . braise it." I wasn't quite sure what braising was, but it sounded impressive.

Nicole took a soda from the fridge. "I ate out. You clean up that mess when you're done."

One thing about a person like that—you really savor her absence.

I dug out one of the vegetarian cookbooks Sherman had loaned me. "Oh, heck. Braising is no big deal."

"We were born to be cooks. Chefs. Caterers!" I said, after the first tofu nugget.

It was, in fact, such a splendid dinner the twins ate steadily without even doing bizarre things to their food.

"I guess we should have told your sister about the Chinese Men's Students' Yoga Olympic Swim Team," I said, over raspberry sorbet.

Laurelle didn't hesitate. "Nah."

"It's pretty interesting."

"I know."

"Are those men going to swim for the party?" Aida asked.

"Dez!" Laurelle gasped. "You don't suppose they plan to practice tomorrow?"

It hadn't occurred to me that they might. "I don't know how we'd reach them."

There was no Fong Li in the telephone book, nor did information have a number listed in his name.

"What if they just show up?" Laurelle worried.

"Maybe they'll swim and leave before the company gets here."

"But what if they come *during* the party? We can't just tell them to go home. It's sad enough that all we can do for people who stood up to a rotten government is let them use a *swimming* pool."

"Are they going to wear clothes to the party?" my sister asked.

At bedtime, Laurelle worked so much setting gel into her hair I was worried that she might get permanently gelled to the pillowcase.

I couldn't help thinking that somewhere out in the night was a man who'd leased our pool to the swimmers. I reminded myself that we had three large, boisterous dogs with tremendous barks—plus Dow Jones, who could depress any intruder right off the premises.

And there was always Nicole. She could dazzle a prowler with her beauty and then paralyze him with the depth of her character and intellect.

"Can you imagine when we tell everybody we went out to eat with *Mike Harbinger*?" Laurelle marvelled. "And when we tell them he was here almost all Saturday, they will die. They will just die. That's a million times better than having the lead in the school play, even."

"Laurelle, I'd take it easy on that sculpting glaze. You don't want your hair to look like pottery tomorrow."

She daubed blemish cream on her chin. "I remember I thought it was so corny when you said he was a nice guy. But he is. I mean, somebody that gorgeous, and famous, and he's really your friend."

"Sure. Gorgeous, and famous, and nice, and practically *groveling* for your sister. How do you figure it?"

I'd never had a friend spend the night before.

It's funny. As you lie there in the dark, you have an absolute compulsion to share confidences.

"You know," I muttered. "I have to confess, I was pretty hurt that my father would go off and leave us this close to Christmas." No need to go overboard on confidences. No need to add "with your mother."

"Listen," she murmured. "I'm not even going to see my father on Christmas Day."

Yeah, I thought. It could be a lot worse. Anyway, with everything that was happening this weekend, it would be very hard to keep my mind on feeling abandoned.

Right after breakfast Laurelle lay down, on her eyes the chamomile tea bags she'd brought.

"If it's your sinuses or a headache . . ." I began.

"It's so my eyelids won't look puffy," she said. "I have to stay here for half an hour."

The twins had trashed their room, looking for their bathing suits. "You either wear clothes today, and good clothes to the party," I pronounced, "or I will tell Preston and Tran to stay home."

You'd kind of expect, being the guest of honor, that you'd have nothing to do but look good for your own housewarming.

Mike and Preston and Sherman showed up before

noon with leftovers from Sherman's parents' party, plus a carton of sodas and cans of mixed nuts.

"I borrowed a couple of our card tables," Sherman said, "so we can lay out everything by the pool."

Preston went back to the twins' room with them, while Mike carried card tables up to the terrace.

Sherman lingered a moment. "I arranged for Shirley Miller to bring Tran and her mother, so Mike could help us," he said. "I also invited Mike's parents."

"*Why?*" I asked.

"I just felt like it. My folks had a lot more leftovers than I figured anyway."

A maroon Buick wagon pulled into the driveway. Teena got out with Kerri and Marti, all of them carrying cartons. "I didn't tell my folks your father wasn't home," Teena cautioned when I opened the door. "So if I don't see them right away when they come back for us, be sure to get me before they have a chance to talk to him."

"Where do we put the stuff?" Kerri asked.

"We're going to have the party up by the pool!" Laurelle announced, as if she'd just invented electricity. Then she stepped aside as casually as she could so they'd see that Mike was already there.

"A *pool* party in December?" Teena exclaimed. "Fan*tas*tic. Pat Troup can't *help* but put it in the paper!" She caught sight of Mike and fell silent.

Kerri and Marti saw him at the same time.

It was great. Instead of arguing about how everything should be done, they just followed Laurelle's directions, glancing at Mike when they thought he wasn't looking.

I never knew a quieter, harder working group.

While all of them were setting things up by the pool, I came back down to the house with Mike and Sherman for chairs. I could imagine Marti and Kerri and Teena up by the pool shrieking, and Laurelle telling them she'd spent Saturday with him.

Here it was not much after noon, and Nicole had risen.

Sitting in her robe in front of the television, she was holding the remote control in her left hand and polishing her toenails with her right, her foot on the coffee table and her cassette player beside her on the sofa.

She did not look up when Mike and Sherman said hello. She did not speak. Of course, flipping through channels probably required all of her brain cells.

Laurelle directed everybody where to place the chairs on the terrace.

Finally, she stepped back and surveyed the tables, all the food and drinks and plates and glasses. "Okay."

For as long as I'd known Laurelle, I'd noticed that, while she was part of the most popular group of girls in school, she wasn't really at the center of it. Now, having spent Saturday hanging out with Mike Harbinger, up here with me and my swimming pool, she had become a celebrity to her own friends.

Who could blame her for wallowing a bit?

Nicole, in jeans and sweatshirt that probably cost more than her mother cleared in a day at work, came charging up to the terrace. For a second, I thought she'd come to send everybody home. But this was one shaken twit. Nicole Carson was *upset.* "Do you know what those kids are *doing* down there?" She could barely get the words out.

"You all stay here and don't let any guests head for the house." If Preston and the twins could get this much emotion out of Nicole, I realized, they must have done something that could destroy a community, let alone a housewarming.

Ignoring my orders, Sherman and Mike followed Nicole and me down to the house.

In the parlor, behind the sofa, Preston and the twins were working busily, happily, quietly.

Doll stuffing, doll torsos, doll heads and arms and legs, Lego blocks, pliers, Country Herb salad dressing, combs, measuring spoons, rolls of toilet paper, fresh garlic, a tin of cloves . . . I couldn't take in all of the stuff strewn on the rug.

Even Mike was shocked. "What are you *doing*?"

Preston was serene. "Well, we took all the insides out of the dolls and rubbed herbs and spices in their bodies. Then we'll fill them with presents and . . ."

"That is the most sickening thing I ever heard of!" Nicole snatched her electric rollers from Aida. "You're lucky somebody doesn't turn in this whole household! And what are all those kids doing up there by the pool with all that food?"

Appalled as I was by the mummy-making, I was not going to let anybody interfere with my party. "We're having a surprise housewarming."

"Does your father know about it?" she demanded.

"If he did, it wouldn't be a surprise." I was impressed, myself, by how firm and logical I sounded.

I was beginning to understand that this Nicole was so self-absorbed, she simply couldn't cope with intellectual complications. She actually looked uncertain.

"And," I added, "all my father's friends will be here any time now, so you can either help tidy the parlor or go someplace where you don't have to see it."

She considered. I suppose the idea of working when she wasn't forced to was more than she could contend with. *"I'm* not going to have anything to do with any of it. You can clean up after these . . . these monsters. And you'd better tell your father I didn't know anything about this party until just now!" She snatched her tape player off the sofa. Clapping the earphones over her ears, she stormed off to my father's room.

"You get every bit of this stuff out of sight," I ordered Preston and the twins, my voice more deadly than I'd ever dreamed I could sound. "And you stay in your room and out of trouble!"

"What about Tran?" Aida asked.

"When she gets here, you may come out," I assured her, "without any of . . . that."

In the garage, the dogs began to howl.

"Company must be coming," Sherman observed.

"Will somebody shut the dogs up?" I was beginning to feel as frazzled as Nicole.

Sherman and Mike went out to the garage.

It took three trips for the twins and Preston to cart everything from the parlor. I knew I should make them put things like the pliers back where they belonged, but I had a housewarming to worry about.

"Where are we going to bury them?" Preston asked Antony, as if their gruesome work hadn't been interrupted.

"Don't you dare even *think* of burying those dolls in our yard!" I warned fiercely.

"We have to smoosh more herbs and stuff on their outsides and wrap them first," Antony said.

"We'll put the tombs where the company isn't," Preston offered.

"You do not put tombs anywhere in this yard!" I roared. "And pick up those eyes off the floor!"

I was about to impound the dolls when Sherman came in with Mike.

"Dez, most of the company's here!"

It's not easy to compose yourself for a party when you've been confronted by disembowelled toys in your parlor, but walking up to the terrace with Sherman and Mike I told myself firmly that everything would be fine. I was a little nervous, as if I were about to step out on a stage in a part I'd never rehearsed. Me, the *guest of honor*! So what if the dogs were barking and howling again? Didn't Elizabeth Taylor have a bunch of dogs? Didn't Queen Elizabeth have corgis? Didn't their dogs ever bark at company?

As I walked through the gate I saw that the terrace was full of people. Pat Troup was wearing full-cut purple slacks and a heavy gray sweater with green and orange flecks in it. She'd gotten new glasses, so that the right earpiece was no longer held on with a safety pin. I kind of missed the old ones.

Mike's parents were there, along with Ms. Dett-weiler, Aunt and Langley Morris, and at least half a dozen of Mike's friends. Elliot Lofting stood off by himself in glen plaid polyester slacks and a navy blue blazer.

Nobody was talking. Nobody was *moving*.

It was a lovely, clear day. A lovely, clear, crisp day. A clear, crisp, cool day. All of my friends, all of our guests, stood around in coats and jackets and sweaters, flicking furtive glances at the opposite end of the pool terrace, where eight men in tiny swim briefs clustered around three enormous iron braziers full of new-lit charcoal.

"Oh, Dez." Sherman looked at the Chinese Men's Students' Olympic Yoga Swim Team. "You should at least have told them to dress."

Seeing Sherman with Mike and me, Fong Li hurried around the pool to us. "How very kind of you. We are . . . we are deeply crushed."

"Touched," his tall teammate murmured.

"Touched. You shouldn't have gone to so much trouble. And you invited so many of your people to meet us. I promise you, that with such encouragement we cannot help but . . ." He paused, overcome with modesty. "I see your friends are waiting for us to be introduced to them."

I looked at Sherman.

"Oh," Sherman said. "Oh . . . here come Mona and Lisa."

Mona and Lisa stepped through the gate onto the terrace as if they were entering a prehistoric forest rife with dinosaurs.

Lisa wore a brocade coat and a dark blue taffeta dress with a short, full skirt. Her eyeliner and even her eyelashes matched her dress, her hair was as blond as hair can get without being white, and her earrings hung all the way down to her shoulders.

Mona's hair was redder and more bouffant than I'd ever seen it. Under her black bouclé shawl she wore a long, swirling, print caftan with silver threads worked through it.

Not many people would get that dressed up for some kid's housewarming.

If they were nonplussed to see eight men in little swim bikinis along with all our clothed guests, they gave no sign, not so much as a flicker or a tic. The only time I'd ever seen Mona or Lisa display much reaction was when I came to their salon after I got varnish in my hair.

They stood apart, not attempting to mingle.

Not that anybody was mingling.

Mike recovered himself. "So . . . let me introduce everybody." He led Fong Li and the tall swimmer toward some guys from his high school track team.

Mona made her way around the other end of the pool to me. "Is there a bathroom around here? My hose are binding."

Shirley Miller picked her way down the path from the street level, along with Tran and her mother and a couple of people in their forties I'd never seen in my life.

"*Who are those strangers?*" I hissed at Sherman.

"I have no idea," he whispered.

"You start introducing people. Most of them look like figures in a wax museum." Taking a handful of nuts, I led Mona toward the house.

Laurelle trailed us. "Dez . . . if they start swimming, we should be sure to explain to everybody who they are."

As we came closer to the house the dogs drowned out the few sounds from the party above.

"We have to do something about that howling," Sherman, on our heels, advised. "A lot of the guests are looking as nervous as if they'd been invited to the Baskervilles'."

This was not the party I had pictured.

"If I didn't know the animals, I would call it blood-curdling," Laurelle agreed. "We'd better let them into the house before the neighbors start phoning the police."

As soon as I opened the front door, she headed for the garage.

"The bathroom is down the hall, first door on your right," I told Mona.

I'd forgotten to remind Laurelle how our dogs tend to run over people. They tumbled into the parlor, barking, yelping greetings, gamboling, Dow Jones plodding along in their wake.

Laurelle tottered in after them, her hair all unsculpted.

Mona sprinted into the bathroom and slammed the door.

I heard a car pull into the driveway. Laurelle looked out the window. "Dez! It's your father! *Early!*" She grabbed Sherman. "Get out the back door and up to the deck and tell everybody he's here! Make them hide, quick! Not a sound out of anybody until we bring him up there. Then everybody jump out and yell *Surprise!*"

"You wouldn't happen to have any antacids?" Mona stepped out of the bathroom, then flattened herself against the hall wall as the dogs scrambled past her into the twins' room.

"Check the medicine cabinet," I advised.

There was the sound of another car. Still at the

window, Laurelle drew back the curtain again. "Oh, wow! Oh, bummer! Dez, it's the cops!"

I rushed to the window and peered out.

She was right.

A police car had pulled into the driveway behind my father's car.

Surely they'd just warn us or give us a citation. They wouldn't bust the dogs on a first offense—Dow Jones would never survive a night in the pound. *But what if Herb and Joe and Sadie already had a record for running through the Groves' concrete?*

"I'll stall the police," I told Laurelle. "Go find Mike and Sherman and stash the dogs out of sight!"

As I opened the door and stepped out and closed it quickly behind me, another dreadful thought occurred to me. *What if the Chinese Men's Students' Olympic Yoga Swim Team was not in the country legally?* What if the Immigration Department had sent the police to round them up?

That could really put a damper on a housewarming.

The officers approached my father as he stepped out of our car with Ruth Carson.

"You've got somebody parked up on the street with his lights on," the dark-haired officer advised them pleasantly.

"*AIIIEEEEEYEEEE!*" It was my brother's

scream, a cry so wild, so harrowing, that it stirred the hair on my neck, raised the bile of horror in my throat.

"HELP! NO! STOP!" My sister's shriek was even more ghastly.

Shoving past both policemen, my father and Ruth Carson dashed into the house and around poor Mona, who had just stepped out of the bathroom again.

"They're ripping all their insides out!" Preston shrieked.

Revolvers drawn, the officers charged into the house after my father, past Mona, who remained plastered against the wall.

The door of the twins' room was open, the room empty.

The screams came from outside, moving up toward the terrace.

Ruth and my father dashed out my bedroom door, the police close behind.

"Wait! Wait! Wait! Don't anybody panic!" I scrambled after them.

As we reached the deck level, I saw Herb careering around the pool, between his frothing jaws an armless doll swaddled in layers of toilet paper, streamers of it trailing from its torso.

On either side of Herb, shouldering him, slamming into him, each with slavering fangs clamped around a slobbery wrapped doll, raced Joe and Sadie.

Behind them Dow Jones waddled happily, growling, savaging a plastic doll leg.

It had never occurred to me before just how *realistic* those dolls looked, especially in such a blur of motion.

Shrieking in rage and horror, the twins and Preston pursued the dogs around the pool, around the tongues of flame that licked from the charcoal in the braziers.

The police burst through the gate.

The Chinese Men's Students' Yoga Olympic Team, as one man, dove into the water.

At the same moment, guests leaped out from behind bushes, tables, the diving board.

"*SURPRISE!*" they chorused.

I don't suppose it's something the Police Academy trains anybody for.

"*FREEZE!*" roared the older officer.

I can see how he must have felt, grossly outnumbered, with snarling dogs flaunting hideous prizes, desperate shrieking children, charcoal braziers flaming around a swimming pool in December, undressed men leaping into the water at the sight of

149

him, hordes of people springing out to yell at him.

Everybody froze, except for Preston and the twins and the dogs.

There was no sign of movement under the water.

As Herb ran under one of the card tables, it toppled.

Not a guest moved, but for a few involuntary flinches from those sloshed by sodas or hit by flying refreshments or jostled by Herb.

Most dogs are born performers. Surrounded by this frozen audience, thrilled by the crowd, ours were moved to *entertain*, dodging among the motionless humans, growling and shaking the dolls, letting Preston and the twins get almost close enough to touch them.

I wasn't sure whether "Freeze!" also meant "Don't make a sound!" but I couldn't stand there and see my dogs shot for ignoring a police command.

"It's okay!" I told the officers. "Really! No crime! Nobody hurt!"

"Dez!" Laurelle stared at the water into which the Swim Team had leaped.

There was not a bubble rising.

"They've drowned!" she cried.

That thawed a few people. Shirley Miller dove into the pool, followed almost at once by Langley

Morris, Mike, Elliot, and Mrs. Carson.

The Newfoundland in Joe came to the fore as he dropped his doll and flung himself after Laurelle's mother.

"Hold 'em, Foyle!" The blond officer thrust his revolver at his partner and leaped into the pool.

Politely resisting the people attempting to haul them from the water, the Chinese Men's Students' Olympic Yoga Swim Team struggled to the shallow end and stood.

"We are legal!" Fong Li shouted. "We have asylum!"

"That's right! That's true! And the dogs are friendly!" I cried.

"They've had their shots!" Sherman yelled.

Ruth Carson batted at Joe, who had sunk his teeth in her sleeve and was attempting to drag her into deep water. "Drop me!" she commanded. "Drop me!"

What could I do? I couldn't let my dog drown my friend's mother. I leaped into the pool.

The shock was like a fist in my stomach, and the cold water made me ache all over instantly, but I managed to get Joe by the scruff of the neck. Grabbing Ruth's sleeve, Mike pried it from between the dog's jaws.

"There's no crime," I cried to Foyle as my father seized my collar. "The dogs are just playing with mum—dolls."

From the icy water, Langley Morris asked, "May we come out and freeze on dry land?"

Mr. Harbinger reached into the pool to grab Mike. *What is going on here and how are you mixed up in it?"*

"You take your hands off my son!" Mrs. Harbinger flared.

Sherman helped Shirley from the water while Laurelle helped Joe clamber out.

There were shrieks from the guests near Joe as he shook himself. Drenched by our dog, Foyle held his ground, and his gun.

Ruth Carson climbed from the water, followed by the blond officer.

Our dogs had never been taught "Freeze!" And they were much too excited to even hear "Stay!"

Skidding around the wet coving, Herb slipped. With a phenomenal dive, Aida tackled him. Preston grabbed the doll's shoulder stumps while Antony pursued Sadie.

As my father hauled me from the pool, Herb, snarling like a werewolf at bay, shook the doll ferociously. Flung back and forth though he was, Preston hung on.

Growling as fiercely as any beast, my sister clung to the dog. With a dreadful ripping noise, the doll split clear across the middle. Preston fell backwards. Chamomile tea bags, crayons, paper clips, toothbrushes, Nicole's nail polish, and a tube of hemorrhoid ointment spilled from the doll's cavity.

"Oh, that is disgusting," the dripping blond officer said. "You people are a sick, sick group."

Taking his revolver from Foyle, he holstered it.

Foyle holstered his own gun.

Joe seized the doll half Preston had dropped and streaked after Sadie and Antony. No longer held at gunpoint, the guests who'd not been in the pool leaped onto chairs, scrambled up on the retaining wall, even tried to climb the fence as dogs and children dodged, snarling and screaming, among them. I guess nobody dared run for the gate out of some paranoid fear of leaving a crime scene.

Mona and Lisa stepped out on the diving board and sat down, observing the chaos like patrons at an untidy but interesting play.

Preston and Antony closed in on Sadie. As Antony threw his arms around the dog, Preston yanked on the doll's head. It came clean off. Crackers, finishing nails, antacids, sculpting glaze, thumbtacks, several of Nicole's cassette tapes, and Laurelle's blemish cream spilled over the terrace.

Dropping his doll leg, Dow Jones lay down to chew a cassette tape.

"Oh, guy! My sister's earrings!' Laurelle leaped to retrieve them from under the feet and paws.

"Your sister!" Ruth Carson seized her by the arm. "Where is your sister?"

"Everybody! Everybody!" Foyle yelled desperately. "Somebody! Anybody! *Explain!*"

9

T he police let my father and Sherman and Laurelle
and me put the dogs in the garage.

Then they herded us all into the parlor.

They rushed us through the explanation, which
was a relief, since so many of the guests were wet.
The officers left without even issuing us a warning,
as if they were eager to be done with us, or maybe
just to get out of their soggy uniforms.

Most of the dry guests departed without even
stopping to say good-bye.

My father and I gathered up towels for all the
people who'd been in the pool or anywhere near Joe.

While the wetter guests went into other rooms to strip, Mona and Lisa strolled back up to the terrace to see if there was any food not trampled on.

I started for my room to get blankets for Mrs. Carson and Shirley. "Don't go in," Laurelle advised. "Mike and the other guys are changing in there. They'll need more towels."

"No problem," I said. "Bramwell left his bathrobe and a bunch of bedding so Dow Jones wouldn't get homesick."

While Sherman went to fetch the dog's robe and bedding, Laurelle and I took her mother and Shirley to my father's room.

Nicole was on the bed listening to tapes and leafing through a copy of *Allure*.

Shivering, Mrs. Carson tried to wrest a blanket out from under her daughter.

Nicole took notice of us.

Nicole took off her earphones.

"Can we go home now?" she asked. "I am bored out of my gourd here."

I fished out some of my father's jeans and shirts. Sherman took them to the guys in my room, and brought me Bramwell's robe.

I let Shirley have my father's robe, and I handed Bramwell's to Ruth, noticing with some satisfaction that it smelled a little doggy.

By then everybody was out of my room, so I could go in and change.

When I came out, Laurelle had scorched the last of the soy milk trying to make hot chocolate.

The front door opened, and Mona and Lisa strolled in. "Those guys in swim briefs are still in the pool," Mona advised me.

"You can tell them it's okay to come out." I was too tired to contend with anything more.

Lisa shook her head. "They're busy showing some kid named Elliot how to ignore the fact that he's wet."

Mona watched my father lighting a fire in the Swedish fireplace. "Thanks for everything. You people really know how to throw parties."

"Would you call that a happening?" Lisa asked.

As they opened the front door to leave, Mona cried "Yeek!"—the first sign of emotion either of them had exhibited since they arrived.

Bramwell Grove was standing there. He looked only a little surprised to see Mona and Lisa leaving. "Ladies." Then he stepped inside. "So how's my dog, and what's with all the traffic fleeing the place?"

Sherman, good old Sherman, hurried to explain.

Meanwhile, my father went out to the garage.

We could hear him: "Stay! Back! Down!"

"Is he talking to my dog that way?" Sherman's uncle demanded.

"Never," I said sincerely. "Just to our own."

My father came back carrying Dow Jones, who immediately launched himself from my father's arms into Bramwell's.

It was interesting to watch Bramwell Grove struggle to hide his feelings while Dow Jones kissed him from nose to chin and almost wriggled out of his grasp with delight. Still holding the dog, Bramwell made Sherman come with him to check the house and grounds for damage.

"Stay out of the bedrooms," Laurelle advised. "There are people without clothes in them."

"Let me explain again," Sherman told his uncle.

While my father put everybody's clothing in the dryer or on the ironing board, I sagged into a chair.

Sherman returned with his uncle.

"You've done a lot with the place," Bramwell told my father, stroking Dow Jones. "Pool looks great. Only, tell me again, who are the eight guys in it claiming they have asylum?"

"I told you." Sherman was patient. "They're training for the summer Olympics. After they cleaned the pool, we let them practice in it, but we forgot to warn them about the party."

"Olympics." Bramwell was thoughtful. "If they

keep my pool up, it's not a bad deal. Once they make the Olympics, of course, they're going to have to thank me publicly and mention some of my projects. I'll write up an agreement. I might also want to sign up that kid who's standing in his wet underwear without even shivering."

I walked out into the yard, Sherman and Laurelle on my heels.

"It would have been kind of nice if your father had helped my mother from the pool instead of just hauling you out," she observed.

"Laurelle, the man has known me all my life. I am his flesh and blood."

"That's what I told my mother. I hope this all doesn't discourage her. If she drops your father, it means I'll be the only vegetarian at our house on Christmas."

"I'd ask you to Christmas dinner," Sherman told me, "but my parents would never go for it."

Mrs. Carson stuck her head out the door. "Laurelle, get your things together. Time to go."

"So, listen," Laurelle told Sherman and me, "I'll call you guys in the morning, after I see how my mother feels. We have the last of the fliers to put up with Elliot, too. I'll try to convince my mom that nothing was anybody's fault and that your father was going to fish her out next."

She went back to the house.

"I had figured that Aunt and the captain would invite us to Christmas dinner," I told Sherman. "That was before Laurelle said her mother was. Now, I don't know if anybody will want us."

"Aunt and the captain care about you," he assured me. "And they can see that your family doesn't have things under control up here. Anyway, if you don't go to Laurelle's, you won't have to put up with Nicole."

I would not have believed that after everything that had happened I could still be surprised.

"She's beautiful," Sherman admitted, "but she's about the dullest person I've ever met. Mike says it's amazing that a great kid like Laurelle could be related to a pill like Nicole."

If people can surprise you all the time, I thought, maybe there was some hope for us. "Sherman, if Mrs. Farisee hears about what a disaster this party turned out to be, wouldn't you think she'd realize how fast and how seriously things fell apart without her?"

"It wasn't a total disaster. I doubt if anybody there has ever had a more interesting time. And who else has a Chinese Men's Students' Yoga Olympic Swim Team still standing in her swimming pool?"

"But do you think Mrs. Farisee might worry about us enough to come back to us?"

Sherman shrugged.

"Let me put it this way, Sherman. Shall you write to her or shall I?"

"If she came back you'd have to give up your room. You wouldn't dare try to put her in the addition."

He did have a point. While I wasn't ready to accept that we might have lost Mrs. Farisee forever, it wouldn't be easy to give up my own room right after I *got* it.

The day was getting cooler.

I saw Bramwell come out our front door and walk down the driveway toward his Maserati, still holding Dow Jones. "Wait till you see what I brought you from Chicago," he murmured, with no idea there were humans within earshot. "This chew toy cleans your teeth and massages your gums while you chomp on it. And a coat. I figure, a dog your age shouldn't be out in winter without one. Plaid. It's flashy, but it suits you. I mean, a dog with your class can definitely carry it off."

As Bramwell put the dog in the front passenger seat and fastened the seat belt harness, Shirley and some of Mike's friends came out of the house and headed up to the street in their own clothes.

At least our dryer worked.

I started back to the house with Sherman. "I'm going to hear a lot from my father about this party."

"You want me to stick around and say none of it was your fault?"

"That would be a very good idea, Sherman. It would take a reckless man to yell at his landlord's nephew."

"No matter how mad he is, just keep remembering that anybody who could live through that party can stand up to anything that comes after."

I slowed down as we came to the front door. "You know, you have to respect Ruth Carson, the way she dived into that pool. In a way . . . in a way I almost hope she doesn't break up with my father."

"You mean over a little thing like leaving her fully dressed in a swimming pool in mid-December?"

"So he respects her self-reliance." I reached for the knob, preparing myself to face my father.

"Hi."

I turned. It was Laurelle, with Mike and Preston.

"We thought we'd hang around to explain to your father that none of what happened was your fault," she said.

"And Preston's going to help clean up the mess." Mike had a firm hand on his brother's shoulder.

"Laurelle's mom says it's okay if I run her home afterward."

As he opened the front door and stepped in, Laurelle hung back with me. "You've got to come with us!" she whispered. "I will just die! How am I supposed to talk to Mike Harbinger?"

"I'll take Sherman aside and tell him to have Mike drop you off first."

"Sir? Mr. Blank?" Mike stepped into the parlor, Sherman behind him.

Laurelle held me back. "No! Then Mike will think I don't want to be alone with him!"

I could hear Mike clear his throat. "Mr. Blank, we want to kind of clear up how . . ."

"How everything happened . . ." Sherman added.

"Laurelle," I murmured, "if I ride home with you, and then Mike has to drive me back here . . ."

"I'll get my mother to drive you home." Laurelle's voice was a low rasp. "I'll pay Nicole to."

I was trying to hear what Mike and Sherman were saying. Then I thought, no, you can't ignore somebody who's given you a housewarming and stayed to face the fallout with you. "Okay. I'll say I have to pick up my homework from your house. Now you want to come in and help Mike and Sherman talk to my father?"

"Sure," she said. "What are friends for?"

Friends are to count on, when they're not driving you crazy. People move on, as my father had said. But I knew that wherever they were, however old I got, I would always remember old Sherman and Mike and Laurelle. Maybe even Elliot.

Walking into the parlor, I realized I didn't even feel hostile toward my father. No matter how interesting his weekend had been, it couldn't compare with mine for mystery and excitement and terror and chaos—at least not until the very end.

It's not all that bad being twelve. If I were forty, I'd probably just want to put my feet up and sleep the rest of the day. As it was, I was wondering how soon after I got a lecture from my father I could figure out with Sherman and Laurelle and Elliot when we'd get the last of our Christmas posters up.

ABOUT THE AUTHOR

Beverly Keller lives in Davis, California. A tireless fighter for animal rights, she shares her home with a pack of large rescued dogs.

The author's comic novels include *The Sea Watch*, an ALA Notable Book, and *Rosebud With Fangs*, about which the *Children's Book Review Service* said, "If the 'Saturday Night Live' writers ever wrote children's books, this exuberant and unfettered fantasy might be the result."

Desdemona and the Blank family have been featured in *No Beasts! No Children!*, a *School Library Journal* Best Book for Spring, and *Desdemona: Twelve Going On Desperate*. Reviewing *Fowl Play*,

Desdemona, School Library Journal said, "In her third adventure, preteen protagonist Desdemona Blank takes a seat among the ranks of the smart and quirky, such as Lois Lowry's Anastasia or Constance Green's Al."